To my co-workers, who helped me in this process and encouraged me the entire way, giving me feedback and embracing my dreams. To my sister Geridan, who has always supported me and shown me love in many ways. To my mother, who allowed my love for reading to grow in an amazing way. To my husband, whose witty remarks can be found here. And to my gorgeous daughter Violet, whose smiles helped me through writer's block.

# The Lies of Others

## O.P. Fleegle

# Chapter 1

When the Night Consumes

The cursor on my laptop blinks at me. Nothing but the title. I can't bring myself to care or focus. I've been sitting here for two hours with nothing to show for it except hunger.

Slamming the top of the roughly pre-owned computer, I shove myself away from the desk. Grabbing my coat off the chair, I leave the tiny dungeon I call home and walk toward downtown. My favorite little dive bar has the best burgers, and I always find a reason to go visit the owner, Ralph.

He's become an adoptive father to me, and he even hooked me up with my small apartment. Even on my days off, I find myself here. It's a short fifteen-minute walk, so why not?

The walk is quick, and I see the usual crowd of regulars. They all light up at my arrival.

Various greetings come. This hole in the wall has become my home since I stumbled in two years ago with a chip on my shoulder and a past that I've left buried for good reason.

The owner, Ralph, should have kicked me out within twenty minutes, but instead offered me a job behind the bar. My co-worker Chris smiles at me as I take my seat on the worn-out bar stool.

"Give up on college yet?"

I flip him off. He's helped me get where I am, and it took many tutoring sessions. There is always humor in me stopping.

The only thing I'm struggling with is the electives. I see no point in Creative Writing 101, but what do I know? My usual drink slides in front of me. I hear him tell the cook to put on my favorite. I smile behind the glass as I drink. A loud crowd enters the bar and I turn to see a group who look like they belong to a frat house. One of the silent regulars grumbles beside me, complaining of the disruption.

They all come up to the bar, ordering fruity drinks for the girls with them. Chris has no idea how to prepare them and we both know it. Throwing the towel he was just using over his shoulder, he gives me a pleading look, begging with his eyes for help.

I tilt back my drink and gulp it down. The alcohol burns my throat. I slam the glass down and jump over the bar. I make complex sugary drinks with over two ingredients. Chris is a lost cause, but it's okay. I notice they have all moved over to the pool tables just as I finish the last one. I grab one of the old beat-up plastic trays and line the drinks up so they won't topple.

Bending down, I place it on my shoulder and make my way to the group. Clearing my throat, they all look at me and smile. Returning the gesture, I announce the drinks, ensuring that I made what they asked for, then walk away. The news buzzes in the background like normal, going on about climate change and recent events. Then everything goes deathly quiet and my attention goes to the screen. A news reporter is outside the CDC.

"Breaking news! It's said the most recent batches of the flu vaccine have been compromised. Those who have recently been vaccinated are urged to visit the nearest hospital promptly for monitoring.

"The contaminants remain unknown, but they say many patients are showing signs of high fever, heightened aggression, lapses in memory, loss of consciousness, and agitation.

"If you or anyone you know has received the vaccine or is experiencing these symptoms, please contact 911. I repeat..."

The lady continues with her report. Chris and I look at each other and my eyebrow goes up, asking the quiet question of "Are you okay?"

The bar quickly returns to the way it was before. Chris returns behind the bar and starts washing out my glasses. I hear the buzz all around, everyone on the same topic. One of the frat boys approaches the bar and sits on the stool in front of me, staring. I turn to him. "Need another rum and Coke?" I ask, drying the glasses.

"Yeah. Did you get that vaccine?"

I stare at him wildly. "No, I didn't. Standing in line all day is not an option for me."

My answer was short and a little too harsh. He visibly reacts with shock. With a hint of remorse, I offer him a small smile.

"Several fraternity members attended. I wonder if I should check in with them." I shrug my shoulders in response. There's no reason for me to add my opinion. Political and religious belief conversations at work are for idiots.

"I'm going to have to keep a broom near the front to chase your ass away if you keep showing up here." A smile grows on my face as I turn to see Ralph on the other side of the bar. He makes jokes all the time about me being here, but what can I do?

"Sorry, old man, I missed your ugly mug too much."

He scolds me, reaching over to shove me, but I move out of the way only a few inches, just to instigate.

He shakes his head, swatting at the air before reaching behind the bar and grabbing another drink, then returning to his table with the reports all laid out.
The night carries until midnight. The frat crowd has slowly dwindled out, and we're cleaning around the joint, getting ready to close. Chris and I tag-team the chairs to urge the customers to pay and get out. Some don't budge, but that's every day. We've turned the TV up to drown out the silence as we work, and a loud warning system blares and draws our attention.

"Breaking news!" A reporter dressed the same as before, a slim woman with hazel hair, stands in front of the local hospital.

"Reports of multiple assaults have come from inside the local hospital, John Memorial. We have an eyewitness that claims she watched as multiple people attacked one another in the waiting room. Here she is."

An elderly woman with long gray hair stands beside the news reporter. The years show on her face. The reporter puts the microphone in front of her and the witness begins.

"Well, hun, I went in because I've been feeling under the weather, and at my age you can never be too safe. But I was at the entrance about to check in and this man comes running out of the doors that lead to the treatment center with a woman on his back. They were both covered in blood and I could have sworn she took a chunk out of him! It was the worst thing I've ever seen. The man couldn't get her off him! I didn't see what happened to her because I hightailed it out of there!"

The reporter mutters a thank you and continues with the events that have been happening all throughout town. She urges the public to stay indoors when a man flings himself on her from the side.

She screams so loud I think it's going to bust the speaker. A fountain of blood comes from her and the camera drops. The screen cracks on the camera, which shows on the TV. Shoes and jeans are running before two people grab the fleeing person from opposite sides. As they slam him to the ground, another scream breaks out and one man bites into his neck, ripping his throat out. They continue to rip him apart, making the gruesome scene worse, and we are horrified, our eyes glued to the screen.

I hear gurgling and sharp intakes of breath before the screen finally cuts.

Everyone is silent. No one speaks.

A group of people burst into the bar, a few unfamiliar faces are with them. Two of the boys are carrying someone and throw him on the pool table, then slam the door shut and lock it. They put their backs to it, panting. The body they put on the pool table is bleeding from his arm. It looks like something took a chunk out of it.

Shaking my head as a reset, I speak up. "What the hell happened?" I run to the bar and grab one of the clear liquors before going to the table. The guy is bawling his eyes out.

"Some guy attacked Beth and Ryan stepped in. The guy turned around and took a chunk out of him! All we could do was grab him and run. We barely got away! Who the hell does that? What the hell is going on with this place? It's chaos outside!"

His chest heaves as he tries to catch his breath. Ryan, as his friend named him, screams out in pain and we all look down at him.

"Grab his shoulders and keep his arm straight. This is going to hurt." They nod their heads and prepare themselves to do as I say. They both wear a concerned look.

I pour the liquor into his wound to sterilize it. Ryan tries to jerk away and screams, sweat pouring off him.

I pull off my shirt and rip it in two. "Give me that pool stick." I point and Chris runs over, tripping over his feet in the process and brings it over. I bust it over my knee and use my shirt to prepare a tourniquet.

"This is going to hurt. Hold him still!" They both have worried looks but nod at me. Taking a deep breath, I turn the stick once, twice. I wrench it tight slowly, stopping the pump of blood.

Using the other half of my shirt, I bandage up his arm as best I can. Ralph looks at me with a strange look of pride. And Chris is just staring at my chest that's now on display. One girl sneers at me, oblivious to the fact that I did it to save her friend.

"His arm is done unless we can get him to a hospital. This will keep the rest of him alive hopefully, but he's sweating bullets. Was he sick before this?" They all stand there, shocked. I snap my fingers in their direction.

"HEY!"

They can't seem to look away from their friend, and I can't blame them. He looks like death.

Throwing my hands in the air, I walk off to the bar, trying to get my hands to stop shaking. The only people left here before this all happened was the quiet regular who was now helping the frat boy, Ralph, myself, and Chris.

There are three girls and four guys. One girl has placed their injured friend in her lap, stroking his hair as he whimpers quietly, sweating bullets.

"Okay, so we know the hospital is a no-go. We all saw the news. So what are we going to do?"

I scratch the back of my neck; my nerves are going crazy. It's chaos outside.

Without a definite plan, all we can do is wait. Chris has turned on the radio to the local station, but the buzz of static is all I can hear.

"If they do a broadcast, I'd rather be able to hear it," is all he says.

Ralph hands me a shirt and I thank him before throwing it on. The enormous size hides my figure. The shirt is black with a fading band logo on it. I rest my hand on his back for a minute, say a quiet thank you again, then walk over to the girl and the man who was attacked. She's talking to him quietly and I check his pulse. His heart rate is through the roof, he wiggles in pain and whimpers. His body is still engulfed in a fever.

As I turn away, I hear a meek voice. "Thank you." I turn to look at the girl. Her eyes are bloodshot from tears.

I nod and place a hand on her shoulder before I take my leave. This makes no sense. I can only think of one thing that could have caused this, but it's not possible. Deep in my thoughts, I'm pulled away by a hysterical cry. I look for the source and find the girl I just spoke to lightly slapping Ryan on the side of the face. She's almost incoherent as I walk back over.

"I— I don't know what happened. He breathed deeply and then he wouldn't respond."

When I glance at the man, I can see that his breathing is shallow, almost non-existent. I tried to find any signs of a pulse in his neck, but there was no sign. I take a step back and observe Chris while shaking my head. He is gone. I returned my gaze to the woman and placed my hand on her shoulder. I whisper the news.

"I'm sorry, hun, his pulse is gone." She wails loudly, and the mood drops even more, which I didn't know was possible.

The guy from before that tried to chitchat with me walks over. "Are you okay?" I look up at him with a questioning look. "You're covered in blood." He points this out to me, and I look down. I *am* still covered.

"I, uh, yeah, I'm going to go wash up quick. Sorry." I walk to the employee entrance and slam open the bathroom door. The dim lights flicker on as I scrub my hands, arms, and face. I scrub until the water runs clean. Looking up into the mirror, splashing cold water in my face, I see my blonde hair still sits in the French braid from earlier. My rose plump lips look swollen from biting the bottom. My gray eyes stare back at my high cheekbones. I'm attractive by all means, but the tattoos on my arms going up my neck give the appearance of masculine qualities. The shirt Ralph gave me hangs loosely on my five-foot two-inch frame, covering my torso like a loose dress, down to mid-thigh. The worn-out blue jeans have some red splotches on them, but I choose to ignore them.

Muttering under my breath a silent prayer, I open the door. One of the frat boys stands outside. I smack straight into him, causing me to stumble back.

"Are you okay?" he asks. All the alarm bells go off in my mind, sending me into a panic rage. Shoving him off and storming out of the hallway, I kick the door open, leaving him standing there.

The girl who I guess was the dead guy's girlfriend is sitting at the bar now, clinging to someone. She's still bawling, and I give a sympathetic look to him. Tony, the only regular who was left, goes around and rechecks all the windows and doors. I walk up to the bar and pull myself up to sit on the edge.

I clear my throat to grab everyone's attention. "What the hell is going on?" My voice breaks the quiet mourning that has taken over the place.

One guy speaks up, "We should wait and see what's happening."

"We've heard no new updates from the news. Those people who attacked must be insane."

"Did you all see the news earlier?"

"Let's stay here as long as we can because it's not safe." Everyone speaks their opinions, and in the end we all agree to stay put, but I can't stop looking at the body covered by a blanket. Someone took a chunk out of him. The hospital is in a panic. We have plenty of supplies in the kitchen. Although, if the power goes out, we're screwed. Biting my lip, all the information races though my head trying to make sense. One guy stares at me as I do. I look up and hold his gaze for a second until he looks away. Everyone is whispering to each other, having their own conversations. We've finally learned each other's names. The one who comforted Mary, the girlfriend of that guy, is Thomas. The one who made me feel weird is Dolton. Then there's Bridget, Savannah, and Luke.

My gaze keeps involuntarily shifting toward the corpse. A sense of dread runs through my body like it knows something I don't. Mary makes her way over to Ryan, gently cradling him in her arms. She whispers something to him, touching her forehead to his. I shift my focus and grasp a bottle, pouring a drink for myself. The clear glass is cold to my touch. Bringing it up to my lower lip, I notice my hands trembling. I take a long gulp, shut my eyes, and allow the sting to engulf me. I try to lose myself in thought.

A scream erupts from the silence. I look over toward the sound. Ryan, who was previously lifeless, aggressively grabs hold of Mary and tears into her neck. The sight of it makes me feel nauseous. The poor girl's wounds are deep, and blood gushes out, creating a horrifying scene. The room is filled with the terrifying sound of her choking, a desperate plea for help as she tries to stop the bleeding from her neck. She falls to the ground with a loud thud; her eyes remain wide open, reflecting sheer panic, terror, so many emotions in one small area. A scream erupts from her lips. I sprint toward her, my body filled with urgency, but abruptly stop as she continues to lie there, her struggle becoming futile. Ryan latches onto her, his grip tightening as she struggles on the cold, hard ground. She begs for mercy, his fingers sinking into her stomach.
With each rip, blood spills out, creating a crimson pool.

My eyes go wide as I watch. Nobody survives that.

I lift my gaze, only to encounter the lifeless and vacant eyes of the monster, once human. He grabs a chunk of his victim and shoves it into his mouth. The sound of slurping and raspy breath fills my ears. I can't tear my gaze away; I'm frozen in place, all the courage I've ever had is gone, and now I'm terrified. He pauses briefly, directing his complete attention toward me. I'm screaming at myself to move, but I'm frozen. He unleashes a guttural scream and bolts in my direction. I automatically move back a bit, quickly figuring out what's going on. I leap over the bar, somersaulting over it with my back. Using my hand, I look for the bat we keep under the bar. My hands are sweaty, but I resist the temptation to wipe them on my jeans. Finally, I make contact with the handle. Gripping it tightly, I pull it out of the mounted spot. Using the position beneath the bar, I swing it forcefully into the side of his head. He tumbles sideways off the bar and onto the floor. I take a few small steps back, noticing the dent on the side of his head, and a wave of disgust washes over me once again. He charges at me, struggling to maintain his footing. I slam the bat against the dented side once again. His body crashes into the shelves behind the counter, causing a few bottles to shatter on the floor. The chaos leaves Ryan's body in a bloody mess, and a putrid smell assaults my senses Despite this, he doesn't falter. He braces his shoulders and lets out another horrifying scream. Swinging the bat against the opposite side of his head, I silence him. He falls to the bottom of the bar, and I climb on top of the old wooden surface. Unfortunately, my footing slips, causing me to fall off the other side, landing on my hands and knees.

The bat rolls in front of me and I quickly scurry to my feet, grabbing it in the process. Running across the room, he climbs over, using his arms to do all the work. He stops once he's halfway over and releases another scream. Rage fills the air as he climbs.

His eyes never leave me. I prepare myself for the attack. My heart feels like it's going to explode and my vision tunnels. The corpse throws himself onto the ground, landing on his stomach, and he crawls toward me. Urgency and desperation show in his movements.

I bring the bat from my side and connect it with his body. Throwing all my weight behind the swing, his body falls to the ground, but as I make contact, the weapon leaves my grip. In my panic, I can only think of one thing to stop him. Lifting my foot, I slam it down, connecting with his head repeatedly. The force makes a sickening crack as it breaks into itself. Blood runs across the floor.

Shaking, I can't stop my assault. The danger is now gone, but I can't be sure. He came back once. What if he stands up again? What if he comes back and kills Ralph or Chris? My boot creates sludge as my thoughts consume my actions. I'm tackled to the ground by Chris and I'm still in a panic. "No, what if he isn't dead yet? He'll kill us!" In my panicked state I start screaming, tears falling down my cheeks.

Chris cradles my head, shushing me to calm me. Realization at what I just did hits fully and I cry louder, looking down at myself. I'm covered in blood. I thrash out of Chris's hold and throw off my boots, chucking them against the far wall. The panic and adrenaline all crash down at once. My body and mind align. Landing on my hands, my body releases everything, and the disgusting sight from before makes it even worse. I puke until I'm dry-heaving.

Bridget shrieks, drawing my attention to her.

"You killed him!"

I look up from where I'm kneeling and all I see is disgust and rage. Some of them avoid eye contact, and others show nothing but a scowl and a glare. "Why— What... I didn't mean to— He just wouldn't stop." I stumble around with my words, unable to form a complete sentence.

She sneers again, her face twisted in disgust and rage.

"He attacked Mary and was going after her to do the same thing. Did you expect her to let that thing rip her neck out as well?" Thomas speaks in my defense.

Moving to stand, my legs feels wobbly, but I manage. It's like nobody noticed, except for Thomas, that Mary's body sits in a puddle of blood. "So now you're trying to intimidate me? You murderer! Are you planning on bashing my head in too?" Her words sting deep, causing me to curl into myself. I took someone's life. I killed someone, no matter how you look at it. My hands are covered in blood, they shake as I examine them, unable to stop staring. I can hear that voice in my head speaking, its volume rising with every passing second.

Ralph speaks, drowning away the thoughts that are trying to surface. "ENOUGH! He was going after her. I didn't see any of us coming to her defense. He wasn't going to quit—I thought the kid was dead, but he wasn't. He killed someone, so stop being so self-absorbed and understand the situation here!"

He had no heartbeat. He died about an hour ago. We all focus on Thomas. "Yo, Thomas, back up," Chris says. Thomas slowly gets up and backs away. We all take a couple of steps back.

"What do we do?" Victoria asks, finally getting a grip on the danger laying feet away.

Tony coughs to get our attention. We all look at him. "We need to get his body out of here and clean up if the thing that attacked him was like that. We can only assume it transmits through bodily fluids. I know Scarlet cleaned his wound, so we need to be careful. Scarlet, you need to wash off, me and Chris will wrap him and take him out back, and the rest of you need to get the blood cleaned up, but be careful. We don't want to get what he had."

We stand there shocked at the calmness in how he said it. Slightly rattled, we make quick work of getting both bodies out the back door and getting everything cleaned up. We all avoid each other, heartbroken and conflicted about what to do. A couple hours have passed by the time we finish, and we address the elephant in the room.

"What if she comes back to life?" Chris asks. We all look toward the door. "Maybe we should just move her away from the door and wait until we are safe."

Victoria gives me a disgusted glare. I respond with a hateful tone. "Just like Ryan, she's dead now. It's simply a matter of survival." Exhausted by Victoria's attitude, I couldn't help but snap at her.

We all stand there for a second before Chris's stomach breaks the silence. "Well, I guess he speaks for us all. It's been at least twelve hours since we all ate, and I'm sure Scar never got her meal. Help me back here, kid, and I'll whip us up something to eat."

We make quick work at making burgers for everyone. Ralph makes me my chicken sandwich with cheese that I never got before the cook disappeared. "What happened to Cook?" I look at him quietly as I gaze at the apron on the floor.

"Maybe he took off at the first sign of trouble. He probably thought all that yelling was the cops, you know. He's never cared for 'em."

I nod, hoping he's okay. We all sit in silence from then on. Many people have huddled up on opposite sides of the room. I go behind the bar, thinking to myself about how we really need to do better cleaning back here. Chris joins me, placing his hand on mine and giving me a reassuring squeeze. We sit there in the silence. Thomas joins us; Chris and I nod to him in acceptance. Sitting on my other side, he crosses his arms. I lay my head on his shoulder. I don't know why I find comfort in him, but I do.

After a few minutes, he breaks the silence. "Thank you." I look at him and my eyebrows move together.

"No one had the heart to do what you did, but I know I couldn't when he went to attack you. We all froze, and you had to do the part no one else could stomach." The explanation has me feeling validated. "Thank you for defending me. I thought I was going to get thrown to the wolves for a second."

I just wish I didn't have to do it. I lay my head back on Chris's shoulder and he shoves me off. I look at him and he sneaks a look at me out of the corner of his eye before slinging his arm over me and hugging me tightly. "I'm glad you're okay." I doze off in between them, feeling safe for the first time in those long, devastating hours.

# Chapter 2

## Never-Ending Chaos

A couple weeks have passed so far, and things haven't gotten better. We've all been coping in our own ways. Ralph has been trying to stay as busy as possible, along with Tony. Chris has become an expert in hide and seek from Victoria: she has been flirting with him non-stop and he does everything to keep away from her.

Sometimes I like to go find him and talk loudly about where he is just to upset him and pass the time. Ever since the first night, me and Thomas have become close, mostly coming up with horrible pickup lines to pass the time. We had checked outside the back door and Mary was gone. We can only assume she got up and walked away, hopefully pretty far.

Savannah got really sick a couple days after, and Bridget got an awful fever. Obviously, we couldn't be so lucky to lose Victoria, but Savannah passed in her sleep later that night. We don't really know why. Dolton and John sit in the corner a lot and whisper back and forth, but I don't know what about. Food is running low, but luckily the power and water is still running, so we've been able to keep clean and hydrated.

The sun went down a few hours ago and there was a weird noise coming from the road beside us, but no one wants to be the one to investigate. Eventually, the power is going to be cut off. We can just hope it's going to be much later.

We've started trying to come up with a plan. Ralph has his truck, Chris has his car, and Tony has his motorcycle. They parked all three vehicles out back in the lot for the building.

The only thing is seeing who's coming with and who's staying. We all gathered around the bar, the map spread out. "We've gotta get out of town at least. It's too populated, and those noises are only getting louder." Planning out the vehicles: "So it will be me, Tony, Scarlet, and Thomas. We'll grab my truck, and then Chris, Dolton, Victoria, and Bridget will go together."

We've made groups of me, Thomas, Ralph, and Tony. Chris will take Ethan, Victoria, and Bridget. Leaving the bike behind is for the best. The question of how bad everything really is still up in the air, and the only way to find out is by checking. After a lot of back and forth, we decide that me, Tony, and Ethan will go up onto the roof to check it out. I'm really hoping these things can't climb a ladder. We slip out the back door and Ryan's body smells godawful. The ladder is right around the corner. We take a moment to look around for any of those things running around.

Bolting to the ladder was easier than we thought. I didn't know I could climb a ladder that fast, but I swear I broke some kind of record. We get to the top and look over the street. The scene is right out of a horror movie. Cars slammed into each other, one drove right into a store on the corner. There is silent chaos all around us. Mary is stumbling across the road, her neck hanging slightly to the left from where Ryan bit her.

There are at least a couple dozen of them wandering around where we can see.

I see the vehicles in the lot all untouched. After a while, we decide to head back in. We make our way down the ladder, waiting to move to the door together. When Tony's feet touch the ground, we all start back to the door. Turning the corner, a loud growl breaks the tense silence—one of the infected is digging into Ryan's body.

Ethan backs up abruptly, knocking me over. I land on my butt and my bat rattles away from me. The infected's head snaps in my direction and Ethan bolts to the door and slips inside, leaving me and Tony to stare at each other. Tony makes a break over to my bat and the infected jumps on me. I use my arm to keep it back from my face and neck. The loud chomping is sickening as it lunges, trying to clamp down.

I feel the blood that covers its front and face slowly drip on to me. It leaks down my arms, onto my shirt, and into my face. Tony takes a hard swing at the creature. As it moves with the blow, its nails grip the side of my arm and rip into me. I hiss at the pain but keep it down for now.

We bolt inside before it can get to us again and slam the door closed, securing it while the infected bangs on the door behind us. Ethan, Ralph, and Bridget all stand there with looks of fear and anger. "What the fuck did you think you were doing?"

Tony explains what just happened and how Ethan left us for dead after he got its attention. Ralph's face twists in anger and he grabs Ethan by the shirt, using it to slam him up against the wall beside the door.

"If you ever put her in danger like that again, I'll skin you alive." He lets go of Ethan and walks over to me. Grabbing a rag from the counter, he wets it under the sink and begins wiping off my face, looking me over for injuries and asking me if I'm okay.

When he gets to my shoulder, the shirt is torn to shreds and it burns. He tells Chris to grab his first aid kit. Three long, shallow scratches sit on my left shoulder, going down my arm. He cleans and bandages my wound and cleans the rest of me off, throwing my newly found shirt in the trash. I put on another one from the lost and found that Bridget went and grabbed, muttering about karma as she hands it to me. Of course, it's a white tank top.

Bridget says they should throw me out to the wolves, but we take a vote, and they all agree to lock me up in the office for a few hours and see if I turn. Grabbing my bat and a bottle of vodka, I say see you later and walk by everyone like it's no big deal. They all stand, shocked. I don't argue or beg; I can only do what I would want someone else to do. But on the inside, I'm listing my regrets, remembering my past. Making my way into the office, I close the door after me. There is a sofa at the side of the room, and I sit down on the edge, slouching into the old piece of furniture. If my father could see me now, I can already hear the lecture on proper etiquette, how a woman should present herself. I huff to myself and shake my head. That monster still invades my mind even now. I flick off the bottle top and drink it straight. The burn reminds me I'm alive and I sit enjoying the feeling.

Chris stands at the door with a blanket in his hand. He throws it beside me. "It's only for tonight. Once they see they're just being assholes, we'll have you sleeping on the cold floor in no time." He drinks with me, saying something about how only alcoholics drink alone. We go over the past and how we met, how baffling everything is, and he's sorry he wasn't there to stop Ryan. After a while, I get tired. Chris seems to take note as he slaps his thighs and raises up. He tells me good night and that he'll see me in the morning, but I see sadness in his eyes. We all have the same fear, but at least he's pretending for my sake. After ensuring I have enough liquor for the night, he walks out, closing the door behind him, leaving me to lie on the couch with half a bottle left. My mind and body feel like they're floating. Swaying my body with my thoughts, I sing a soft melody to the bottle to keep myself calm:

Well, what is this that I can't see?

With ice-cold hands taking hold of me.

When God is gone, and the Devil takes hold.

Who'll have mercy on my soul?

O Death, O Death, consider my age.

Please don't take me at this stage

I sing the lyrics I can remember from the track my mother adored before she went into a new life all those years ago, leaving me in the care of my father to fend for myself. My eyes drift down and become heavy, and my arm falls slack with the clear liquor in my relaxed hand. I hum the rest.

# Chapter 3

## Change Kills

*Stepping off the bus with everything I've collected in a trash bag, I look around this small town about two hours from the closest city. It's perfect. Nobody would know it exists unless they grew up here. Taking off down the road, I see a shitty little bar shoved into the corner of the street sitting all alone. Hiking my bag over my shoulder, I open the door. Stale cigarettes and peanuts enter my nose, and I take a deep breath as I head straight to the bar. A man is standing there. He's flirting with a guy, and I stare at him. He dabs the man's arm to tell him he'll be right back. Taking my order, he's quick to comply, and I thank him before throwing it back and consuming the whole beverage.*

*The burn runs down, and I feel it warm the path it just traveled. Enjoying the company of me, myself, and I, I look over to see an average man coming my way, stumbling slightly. He places an order and rests his hip against the deep brown bar, then looks at me and tells the bartender to make it two. As he places them in front of him, he slides one across the bar at me. It spills on my shirt and pushes my drink to the side. I stare down at my now-empty glass, not acknowledging him. He snaps to get my attention*

*When that doesn't work, he walks and stands right next to me. I smell the alcohol coming off him in waves.*

*"Hey, sexy, why don't you take off that shirt and I'll clean it for you," he says, slurring his speech slightly. I don't give him a single second of attention, and I can see his face tick slightly at this.*

*"That's cold, you know. When someone buys a pretty girl a drink, the least they can do is smile."*

*I look at him and force the fakest smile I can.*

*"Oh, you're a smart-ass bitch, huh?" he says through gritted teeth.*

*Before he can react or continue with his incoming line of insults, I take the drink he slid to me and slam it into his face, dazing him. Taking the front of his shirt, I use it to slam my head into his, causing him to stumble back and crash into a table, out cold.*

**I blink.**

*I'm at my old home, the one in the mountains that my mother loved so deeply. Sunlight pours in through the open windows. Sitting at the breakfast bar in the kitchen, my mother is singing along to a slow but upbeat tune, her golden blonde hair cascades down her back in loose but perfect curls, her light blue sundress hugs her figure and flows gracefully down. Her singing is like a lullaby.*

*I rest my head in my tiny hands and stare at her with wonder. She turns around and her face is smooth but blessed with smiling lines. Her eyes crinkle in the corners as she looks at me. She pulls me off my stool and sways me with the upbeat music.*

*Twirling and giggling, we dance around the small cabin space. We push away from each other and pull in, out and in, out and in. Her laugh echoes around the room, combining with the music and my own young joy.*

**I blink.**

*Blackness consumes me.*

*Hard leather straps tug at my wrists. I'm sitting on my knees and there is no light. I try to pick up my wrists but struggle.*

*A door opens and light floods inside. A man is standing there; the light hides all his features, but I know exactly who he is. He taunts me with my name.*

*"Scarlet, darling."*

*I try to pull myself free, but I have no leeway.*

*A scream breaks out of me. It feels as if it's tearing my throat apart from the inside.*

**My eyes clamp shut.**

I shoot up from where I'm lying, continuing the scream.

I hear a slight crack from beside me and there is a single spider crack at the top of the bottle reaching down.

I drop the bottle and hold my hands to my chest; tears are streaming down my face. I quickly clear them away before I fall back on the couch again, looking at the night sky through the window. It's almost pitch-black. The stars supply a beautiful scene, but no light.

I take a long swig from what's left in the bottle and sit on the floor. I think of anything to keep from those dreams. Hours slowly crawl by before the sun rises. I feel a slight hum of pain in my shoulder, and I peek inside the bandage, expecting to see an angry, infected cut. I glance down and there is nothing. I unwrap my shoulder and there is blood on the bandage, but the scratches have healed. It's only been a day, but it's already healed over.

I stand up and walk to the door, opening it, the door creaks. I peek my head out and look both ways at Chris, asleep against the wall. Taking his bottle of liquor, I walk past him to the bathroom. Flicking on the lights, I look pale—pale, but alive— and my eyes almost look more vivid.

My hair is a mess. Taking out my braid, I shake my head, letting it fall. I turn on the shower and let the water warm, stripping out of my clothes. I wash my hair and body with Ralph's three-in-one shampoo. I smell like a man. I turn off the water and stay still, listening to what's going on. I watch as the colors combine and go down the drain. I sit in the water for a minute, enjoying it, letting the warmth soothe my aching muscles. I wish I could stay here forever and a day. Taking a deep breath, I open my eyes just as the lights flicker around me. There's a loud thunderous boom, and a second later, it feels like the building shakes.

The lights all cut out at once. "Shit." I feel around, looking for my towel. My hand traces along the wall where it should be, and finally, after a few failed attempts, I feel the fluffy heaven. I bring it into the shower with me and dry myself off in the pitch-black dark, which is harder than I thought it would be.

After a thorough check, I gather my clothes from the floor, hoping I didn't forget my underwear. I readjust my towel, making sure it's wrapped securely around my chest. I open the bathroom door and the hallway is not much better, the only light that illuminates my path is the morning sunlight turning the hallway a pink hue. I use the light to quickly change into my dirty clothes.

As I pull up my pants, I look over my shoulder to see Thomas staring right at me. I let out a slight squeak, and he takes off down the hallway like a child who just got caught. I smiled to myself because of his reaction. Finishing getting dressed, I towel dry my hair as I walk down to the bar. Everyone is gathered in the front. The windows are open. They all go dead silent as I walk in. "I'm alive," I sing out with my arms spread open.

Ralph, Chris, and Thomas all smile at me. Bridget seems pissed, and Ethan is passive. Tony is nowhere to be seen.

"What happened?" I ask.

Dolton is the one to answer.

"We think the power reactor just went out because no one was keeping it. That means that we got to go." He says the last part a little forceful.

Bridget gets snarky. "No, that means we are just without power. You've seen those streets, we won't survive out there."

Ralph interjects, "So, we'll starve in here. At least outside we have a fighting chance."

Bridget and Ralph go back and forth, arguing about what to do. After very valid points made by Ralph and some ear-shattering whines from Bridget, we finally take a vote. Everyone except Bridget votes to leave. We plan to gather anything useful and chart a path to get the hell out of this town. Quickly tying my hair up with my ponytail holder, I ensure we have everything we need. Going down the list, the supplies are light, but it's all we have after so long.

I grab the bat and everyone else has their weapons. We all go along the back of the kitchen in our groups. Mine goes first, for some stupid reason. I'm leading this parade, and I don't like it. Slowly, we open the door and listen.

They unlock the vehicles from afar and we try to hear for a second. Me and Chris both stick our heads out. It's clear for now. We give the signal, and like all hell breaking loose, we take off running to the vehicles. I jump in the back and so does Thomas. Everyone gets in their vehicles, and we wait for a moment before turning on the truck. The engine revs to life.

And just like we banged a dinner bell, Mary's corpse comes from around the corner. Her skin looks like it's been scratched off in some places, and her hair sticks to the blood on her. She sees the vehicle and lets out a scream toward us. Charging at us, her body slams shoulder-first into the driver's side door and Ralph curses to himself.

We look over and see more infected people rounding the corner. Some take off running like Mary did, while others slowly walk, their arms hanging to their sides. Ralph throws the truck into gear and peels out of the lot with Chris right on our tail. We swerve in and out of the abandoned cars and see the chaos that took place that night; those things are coming out of stores, alleyways, every nook and cranny possible.

I feel my lungs burn. I didn't even realize I was holding my breath. Ralph never stopped, plowing through a few of the bodies. Loud bumps and bangs sound through the cab of the truck.

Once we seem to be clear of most of the chaos, I poke my head from the back seat. Ralph and Tony look at me.

"So, I guess now is a bad time to say I need to pee, right?" My shit-eating grin is flashing, trying to lighten the mood, and Ralph lets out a thunderous chuckle.

"Shut up, smartass." He uses his giant hand and shoves my face back.

"HEY!" I slide into the seat beside Thomas, who's shaking his head silently and laughing to himself. His shoulders rise and fall with a chuckle. I leaned close to his face. "Do you need to pee?" He mimics Ralph's motion and I cross my arms, playfully grumbling. "Last time I check on your bladder."

They all shake their heads at me as we cut through back streets to make our way to the highway. Despite the congested roads, we make it through fairly easily.

Going in and out of the grassy side strip, we've traveled for about an hour, and I've made myself comfortable at the detriment of Thomas. He's playing with my hair as my head rests in his lap and my legs are up against the door. We slowly roll to a stop at what looks like a motel and Chris pulls in behind us.

I groan at having to move, and Thomas opens the door and slides out. I flip out of the seat onto the black pavement. "Why did we stop?"

Tony looks over at me. "We need more gas, and need to figure out where exactly we are heading." I nod my head and walk over to the hood of the truck as they discuss the next move. They converse among men, and I lose interest quickly.

Taking it upon myself to do my thing, I take my bat out of the cab of the truck and walk around. A couple cars are in the lot with us.

I approach them. They're older cars, but there's no telling what they could have. I try the latch on the hood and unhook the security wiring. Without warning, I pull my bat back and shatter the driver's side window, fishing my hand in. I unlock the door and get to work scrounging around.

I find a purse, cigarettes, lighters, ibuprofen, in the front. Walking around and opening the back, just some random wrappers. A jacket. Nothing of any value.

Popping the trunk, I find a gas can, and to my surprise, it is half-full. Also a tire iron, spare wheel, and a half-empty pack of water. I lug my first find back, and Dolton scowls at me. Thomas walks up and helps me while throwing everything in the truck bed.

Proud of my first trip, I go to head back only to have Ethan grab my shirt, almost choking me. I twist around and give him a look. "Could you not be so loud? People might still be around." I look at him for a moment.

"I disabled the security system, I thought that was good enough." Using force, I unlatch his hand from my shirt and throw it back at him. He sneers at me, and the look in his eyes makes me take a step back and grip my weapon tighter. There's something wrong with this guy. His face has switched from a neutral tone to something sinister, and it's sending alarms down my spine. I fight the urge to cross my arms to my stomach. Looking weak in front of him is not a good idea.

The others notice the tension so, I guess to pacify things, Chris walks over and lightly grabs my elbow.

"Nice find, Scar, let's look at what else is in there." He pulls me away and forces me to break the stare down between Ethan and me.

He comes with me to the last two and finds nothing memorable. But I show him what to disconnect in order to keep the alarm from sounding, so that's definitely a win.

I pull out one pack I found and light up as we walk back. I'm not a religious smoker, but I could use the release. Ethan found a garden hose and got to siphoning what gas we need and saving whatever we can for later.

Deciding to head west, we all pile in. The goal is to get as far away from here as possible and avoid cities. The surrounding chaos tells us everything we need to know. So far, we've been lucky, but we can only hope it holds out.

# Chapter 4

## Life on the Road

After so many days on the road, people get mean and quite annoying,.

At the moment, Thomas has made it his mission to piss me off, and he's getting close.

He's now sprawled out in the back seat, snoring like a freight train, and every time I raise my hand to smack him awake, Ralph gives me a stern look in the rear-view mirror.

I offer a sickly sweet smile before lowering my hand and stroking his hair. His arms have found their way around my waist, and I welcome the warmth and comfort from it. Looking down at him, it's quite a fresh look for him. He's become my protector from Ethan due to him targeting me with all the blame and emotional abuse he feels like inflicting. I don't know what I did to the guy, but he hates my guts.

Thomas' features turn soft in his sleep, and if he would just shut the fuck up with the godawful snoring, I'd call him adorable, but the noise takes away a few points on that scale. His muscular body fills in the entire back seat. I wouldn't think with his height he could sleep like this, and he normally is sore when he wakes up.

I've got no idea where we are, but we've only stopped for a couple minutes. Those things pop out of nowhere and we've become accustomed to running. The food is gone and now we just stop to scavenge, hoping to eat. Ralph flicks on his blinker and pulls into an RV camp, Chris follows. When we stop, I slowly slide out from under Thomas, unhooking his arms so he can sleep. He deserves at least that for everything he's been doing for the group and me.

We've made a habit out of what to do. We break off into pairs, but I walk by myself since I'd rather he sleep. Ralph asks me if I'm sure, and I give him a reassuring smile before nodding my head, ensuring I'll be fine. Walking to the far end of the line, I hold my bat in a tight fist. Going alone is a lot more nerve-wracking than I realized. Knocking on the RV, I wait for a moment and listen. When no movements are heard, I open the shiny plastic door and climb the stairs. I'm welcomed with a disgusting smell, and I pull up a bandana I've fastened into a mask to block some of the awfulness.

I walk back to the bedroom. The bed was left unmade, but the flies buzzing around make it even more eerie. There is a backpack thrown on the mess of blankets. Pulling it toward the edge, I shake it, emptying the contents. Items tumble out: camping gear, gloves, a moon pie maker. I throw the junk to the side, keeping the gloves, and sling the bag over my shoulder. Just as I'm about to leave, I see a large black case. Inside is something I haven't used since high school.

A black compound bow with at least 15 arrow tips and a bunch of tools, triggers, strings, different heads, fletching. I run my fingers over the strings. It's a little too large for me, but I can always adjust the weight. I throw my hand in the air, proud of my find. Searching the cabinet, I find some saltines and canned food.

Throwing them all in the pack, careful of the arrows, I grip the bow tightly as I exit the camper. Deciding my find is good enough, I make my way back to the truck. As I'm closing the space, a loud scream rings out to my left. My head snaps sharply toward the noise—in the distance, Victoria is running toward us with what looks like a dozen dead ones following her. I freeze.

I know she will not make it, but I need to make it before her. I bolt to the truck, hoping to at least survive. Tony and Ralph are already inside. I see them looking around; hopefully, for me. They are yelling something from inside the cab, but before I can make it past the RV corner, an arm reaches out, swiping at me.

I throw myself sideways to avoid it, and a woman in a stage of decay growls at me. I step back, my eyes snapping between the stumbling infected and Ralph. He keeps yelling something, but I can't hear him or make it out in the slightest.

I take three steps back but keep my balance, unable to drop the bow or to grab my bat from the pack. I can't do anything to get to them. Three more round the truck from the other side. Two have turned their attention to the engine bay, scratching and slamming their arms at it, trying to get to the noise inside.

Victoria is nowhere to be seen. I keep taking step after step back, trying to find an opening, but there isn't one.

"JUST GO! I'LL FIND MY WAY OUT!" I yell, and Ralph yells from inside the truck, staring at me in horror. We lock eyes, and I can see him demanding I get to the truck.

Tony has more of a survival sense in this moment and slams on the gas, sending the truck forward with force, crushing the ones that were targeting the hood. The ones who were on their way turn toward the truck, so I take the opportunity and run for the trees. Pushing my legs to go faster, arms pumping, throwing the bow over my head to sit on my shoulder across my chest. My lungs feel tight as I hit the tree line, but I don't stop.

Branches and bushes scrape at me, and I feel the minor cuts forming. After a few minutes, but not for long, I stop to organize myself and try to plan. I slam the bag down on the ground and pull out the old, weathered bat. I sling the pack back on and look around. My throat is dry and hot from running, and I struggle to gulp down much-needed air. I bend over, putting my head between my knees. I focus on my breathing. My chest is heaving fast, and my lungs feel like they can't fill.

I really should have done more cardio before all this crap. I hear a scuffle in the distance, and my head snaps at the sound. A lone dead one charges at me. Luckily, it hasn't let out one of those awful screams yet. I prepare myself for the conflict, bringing the bat up and swinging hard. It falls to the ground. Using all my force, I bring the weapon down hard; it only takes a couple swings before its skull cracks open. A putrid smell fills my nose, and my mouth waters in response. Throwing up all I had in my stomach right beside it, I use the back of my hand to cover my nose and stumble off.

Not taking the time to look around, I bolt farther into the trees. Leaves crunch under my shoes, and I feel the sting of the small cuts on my skin. I push myself harder, making it feel like I've been running for hours, but I know it's only been about five minutes. I slow down and look behind me, to my left and my right. I hear nothing, and I can't see anything but trees. When I started running, I went at an angle, so if I head to the left, I should hit the road sooner rather than later and end up right on the escape path.

I walk to the right, hoping I'm not wrong. Counting my steps to help the time pass is boring the hell out of me, but it's all the entertainment I have for now.

My focus leaves me as I hear the sickening crunch of something being chomped on, followed by a sharp intake of breath. Looking over to my right, a dead one is gulping down a deer but hasn't noticed me.

I drag my steps, keeping an ear out for it, making sure it's still content with poor, unfortunate Bambi. Keeping my eyes focused and on a swivel, forgetting the counting game that was helping me pass the time, I get away from the sight without raising an alarm. It seems I didn't run too far into the woods because before long, I'm back on the road.

Following the direction I assume they'd go in a hurry, I walk in the center of the road, bow in hand, arrow at the ready. Watching the sun slowly move in the sky gives me reason to worry. I've got little to no sense of direction and winging it is my only hope, although sadly I normally couldn't find my way out of a wet paper bag.

After what feels like hours, with my feet sore and most likely blistered, I see a glimmer of hope. An old motel sits like an oasis. There are a couple cars parked and forgotten. The old sign no longer gleams, and the board's date hasn't been changed since I guess it started for them here. I check one door, and it's a simple key. Of course it's locked. I can only hope the front office has them. I know I have to find one before I lose all the sunlight. Simple enough, right?

Opening the door to the front desk, I used my foot to prop it open, bow drawn and ready. Stepping in, I feel the door close behind me as the draft slowly disappears.

Making my way over to the old vending machine, my mouth waters at all the goodies left inside. I brace my back against the cold metal and slam it, creating a loud noise.

One, two, three, three knocks, no noise or dead thing has made itself known. Slowly, I unload my arrow and walk over an old corkboard that has all the room keys on it except for a missing few. I grab one on the top level—234. Putting my bow away, I grab my bat and walk to the vending machines. Seeing all the goodies makes me let out a tiny squeal of excitement.

I pull back my bat and take a swing. Fortunately, it's old enough that it shatters after a few hits. Hastily stuffing everything into my pack, I examine the assortment of newfound treasures: peanut butter crackers, chips, chocolate, and Slim Jims. After sealing it shut, I swiftly ascend the stairs to the room I've selected. Upon entering, darkness engulfs the space. I search the room for any sign of disturbance. To my relief, everything appears perfectly untouched. You can see the parking lot from the window.

The curtains are closed. I lock both the doorknob and the dead bolt. I move the old, out of style dresser, pushing it in front of the door, and make sure my barricade will hold. There are two queens in the room. I drop my bag and bow, flip on my flashlight, and approach the small bathroom. Slowly opening the door, there's nothing but a sink, toilet, and empty shower. Thank goodness, luck is finally on my side! Letting out a slow breath relieved at the sight, I walk in and turn the shower knob, a rattling in the pipes come to life, making me debate dancing for joy. Not wasting another minute, I jump in, clothes and all, and scrub away all the dirt and grim I've collected, using the little bar of soap on the sink to clean my hair. After I know my clothes are clean, I strip them off and wash myself. The water is freezing, but it feels great to just feel clean. After a couple minutes, my skin has tiny goosebumps all over it and I can't take anymore freezing water, so I jump out and wrap myself in a towel that hangs near the door.

I set my clothes out on the tile, hoping they will dry quickly. I feel all my energy leave and I feel drained. Losing all the food back in the woods really sucked. Dragging myself from the bathroom, this entire day has been too much, and I feel it in my limbs. I get on the bed, pull the covers up over my lap, and drag my bag over to me. I flick off my light to keep people from seeing me. I devour the jerky and chips, gulping down from the water bottle I had. Feeling full for the first time in about two weeks, I fall back onto the bed, arms open, knowing I can't do anything during the night. Sleep consumes me quickly.

I wake up to the sun pouring in through the curtains. Somehow my clothes had dried in the night. Putting them on, they are stiff, but I'll take whatever I can. Throwing a braid into my hair, I grab my belongings and refill my bottle from the sink. I adjust my bat so I can easily grab it and the arrows. Bow in hand, I peek out the curtains and everything seems clear. Moving the dresser back to where I found it, I unlock the locks and open the door, drawing my bow and sweeping from side to side. A feeling of relief sinks in as I see no danger. Going down to the parking lot, I look through all the cars, trying to find anything useful. One car has a purse in the seat, and it looks like some clothes as well. Unplugging the alarm system, I take a moment and bash in the window.

Quickly jumping into gear, I dump the purse and grab anything useful: some feminine care products, ibuprofen. There's an entire suitcase, so I pull the items out. I grab some underwear that seem clean, a sports bra, some long sleeve shirts, and a heavy field jacket. Putting on the jacket, I sling my bag back on and start down the road. One thing that makes no sense is all the abandoned cars on the road: some have swerved off to the side, some even slammed into trees. Maybe they were infected and that's when it took hold. I'm curious if a crash has the same effect on them as on us. Are they aware of what they are doing at all? Questions run through my mind, with my steps filling in the silence of being alone. I hope they are all okay. I know Victoria didn't make it in time.

A loud boom rings out, and the tree next to me explodes. Throwing myself on the ground and looking at the impact, I see a large black truck coming down the road. Two men are in the bed looking at me. I stare for a moment because it sounds like they're saying something.

"There's a third!" Not understanding what that means, I take off in a sprint down the road. They continue to yell at me, and whoever is driving seems to have sped up. I take a left into the surrounding woods to avoid them. I hear the truck slide to a halt and the doors closing. Multiple footsteps come charging in my direction.

I take aim and let an arrow fly as a warning. It slams into a tree beside one of the men's heads. He turns to me and smiles. "She's a feisty one." I bolt the opposite direction, my feet pounding the ground, crunching leaves and twigs. I can hear them yell, trying to tell me something; I look back for a second to see if I can spot anyone following me. I look forward again and dodge a tree in the nick of time. I keep the pace. My vision shaves a black ring around it and my lungs feel like they have opened.

I lean forward to get more leverage. When one of them comes into my field of vision, he yells, signaling where I am. I slide under a log to avoid having to slow down and keep going, putting my bow onto my body. I pick up my pace, using my arms to drive me forward faster. I slow down. I can't see any of them, but then again, all I can hear is my heartbeat in my ears. My breathing muddies my senses. A loud boom rings out, and the tree next to me explodes. Something shattered it. I crawl away to build into a run, but in my panic, I don't notice a man running up to me until his foot slams into my side, sending me sideways. Letting out a cry as the pain explodes at the point of contact, I look up.

Your average jock stands there with blonde hair, cargo pants, and a red shirt. He has a neutral look plastered on his face and he reaches down for me. My bow is out of my reach. I turn over and try to stand. The ache in my side makes it harder. He kicks me in the ass, and I fly forward with a thump. I turn onto my elbows and face him, looking for any kind of reaction.

"Just let me go. I'm sorry about the arrow thing. It was a joke, and you got me back, ha-ha funny, right?" My voice is uneasy. I lift my right arm to shield myself. He just stares at me with this look I can't pin. Two more people come running up, filling the area behind him.

"Holy shit, man, you actually caught up to her." I slowly inch back, trying to get to my weapon. They look down at me, and the guy in front finally speaks.

"Well, I say she's okay." I can only assume what he means. I shoot toward my bow. My hand gets a grip on it, and I use it as a bat, slinging toward his legs.

I take one out and he yells out a curse as he flies forward. His body connects with the ground and I try to scurry away from the mass of a man. I feel something wrap around my ankle and I'm being pulled backward. I claw at the dirt and dead leaves, trying to get some traction, but get except dirty nails. I flip around onto my back and see he's dragged me underneath him.

He slams himself down and knocks the wind right out of me. He pins my wrist beside my head and takes in my face that is now undoubtedly covered in dirt; so much for my shower. "Sorry about this, but it's for a good reason." He lifts his head and slams it into mine, and dark spots appear in my vision.

My head throbs from the shock of pain and the world slightly tilts. He gets off me and the pressure leaves my chest. I pull at the ground, trying to claw away; my arms one after another pull me closer to my target. A ringing in my ears makes my head throb even worse. A boot enters my view and what I assume is a kick slams into my head, causing a quick moment of pain rather than blackness.

# Chapter 5
## New Beginnings Suck

Slowly waking up, I feel the comfort of a vehicle moving. I'm warm and leaning up against someone, their heat providing comfort to my aching back. Opening my eyes, they sting from the surrounding sunlight. I see two legs around mine, cargo pants and black boots. Strong arms hold me from behind. There's a blanket slung over me. I relax, thinking I'm in Thomas's arms, but it takes a second for everything to come back. I go to throw myself away from the unknown body when he tightens his grip. My arms get trapped at the elbows and I try thrashing and throwing myself in every direction. I knock the back of my head into his face and he lets go of me. I quickly retreat to the door and jerk on the handle, expecting it to open, but of course it has a freaking child lock. I push my body against it only to be met with a wall. Turning around, I probably look like a scared wild animal caught in a cage. I see the man who attacked me holding his nose.

The front seat has the other two, and there's one other guy riding in the truck's bed. The guy in the front turns around, staring at me, his hands in a low open position, telling me to calm down. "It's okay, little lady, you're safe," the stranger says. "What's your name?" It takes a moment to register what he's asking me, but I want answers and I'm not telling them a thing until I get them.

"What the hell is going on?" I ask them through gritted teeth. "One minute I'm trying to find my friends, the next I'm running in the woods for my life. And now Mr. Handsy has me in his arms like a damn python trapped in a moving truck with strangers. This doesn't feel very safe to me!" As if it just dawned on them and the puzzle just clicked into place.

The one I busted in the face curses under his breath. "No wonder you shot at us. I didn't even think about that."

I look at him in shock. "You acted like you were going to skin me alive and knocked me out!"

The person driving shakes his head and lets out a sigh. "I'm sorry, little lady. We didn't want you running into the large group of biters, and we were concerned you would run straight to them. Our approach could definitely use some work." I roll my eyes and cross my arms, muttering under my breath about basic manners. "Well, how about we introduce ourselves and then you tell us your name. I'm Owen, that's Jack, and the one you've attacked twice now is our big softie Jacob. The guy in the truck's bed is Markus."

I eye them all suspiciously. "I'm Scarlet." My answer is short and to the point.

Owen smiles at me. "All your stuff is in the back with Markus. You were knocked out for about 8 hours. We were scared Jacob killed you. That's why he was so close to you, trying to comfort you and make sure you still had a pulse. He felt awful about how he acted."

I look at Jacob and he tries to avoid my gaze. His nose is bleeding, and I crawl over to him. He pins himself into the door, but lets me move his head, feeling the bridge of his nose. The cartilage is fine. "I didn't break your nose, but I'm not sorry. You need to learn that you don't chase women through the forest."

Taking the bottom of my shirt, I wipe the blood away. It's already clotting, so that's a good sign. My eyes flicker up to his and it almost looks like he's blushing. I return to the corner I was in. "So where are you guys heading anyway?" I ask.

"We heard over the radio about a military base for survivors. We're heading there to at least get some answers about what the hell happened." I cross my arms and look out the window. At the very least, I can hitch a ride till they throw me out of the truck.

I've been going in and out of sleep for the last several hours; somehow I've curled into Jacob and he doesn't mind how we've ended up. When I woke the first time, I apologized and he just took my head and laid it back onto his shoulder. I was uncomfortable, but I've grown accustomed to his heart, so I'll take it where I can get it I guess. After drifting back to sleep, I'm woken up by him gently nudging me awake. He speaks so softly it's like a lullaby.

"We're going to stop for a while, take a minute and stretch." He opens the door and I follow. We're at a gas station. This one looks untouched by all the chaos.

"Where are we?"

Owen speaks up from beside me. "We are just about to cross the West Virginia border into Pennsylvania." My eyes grow wide. When this all happened in my little town, we were in Louisiana. I don't know where everyone has gone. I shake the sadness out of my head and look around, walking over to the gas station. I pass Jack and Marcus getting fuel out of the buried container below the pumps. They do quick work of getting the grate off and siphoning the gas into large containers.

I peek into the station. The lights are out, but the place seems untouched. Opening the door, a small bell rings. Waiting to see if anything pops out of the dark with the silence filling the void inside the store, I decide it's safe enough taking the direct path. I make my way over to the counter. Grabbing two plastic bags, I walk the aisles, grabbing beef jerky, chips, bottled water...just your everyday survival needs. I find my way back to the counter and jump over. Seeing the array of bad decisions, I give in and grab about 10 packs and a handful of lighters and throw them into their own bag. Making sure I've collected enough food and plenty of water for everyone, I return to the truck. The guys are still busy at work, and I take my hard-earned findings and throw them onto the floorboard.

I debate going back, but decide against it. Being greedy will only doom someone else. I see Owen walking around; he seems to be the friendliest of the four. He's the best one of any to befriend. He smiles at me as I approach, seeming to enjoy the company. He bumps into me as we walk, cutting me off mid-sentence. "It just doesn't make—" I look down at my feet and bump him as we continue this. We giggle like children, becoming more and more aggressive with each hit. Before long, we've gone from bumping into full-body slamming into each other and the laughter doesn't stop. I pause my walking and let him walk ahead a few steps before charging at him. He surprises me by side-stepping as I pass him, then hooks one arm around my waist and throws me over his shoulder like I weigh nothing. I let out a laugh I haven't heard in a while and brush his back, demanding he puts me down.

"Who raised you?!" I squeal out. He laughs, his body shaking. He answers my question by telling me I've earned what's coming. He walks us over to the truck and I see Jacob and Jack grinning at us. I slightly cock my head to the side, trying to figure out what's going on, when I get moved into a cradle and tossed to Jacob. I squeal in surprise and land with an oomph in his arms. I wiggle out of his grip and make a run back to the truck. Everyone is laughing, and just as I reach for the handle to my safety, Jack scoops me up and turns, throwing me over his shoulder. I can feel his muscular shoulders digging into my stomach. I get a clever idea; grabbing the back of his shirt, I lift it up over his head and cover his face with it, making him forget what he was doing and dropping me. I step back and charge right at him, shoving my body into his stomach and sending us flying into the grassy patch beside the road. I look down; setting my target, I grab his sides. He tenses, and I see my opportunity.

"AH HA!" I yell out in a noise of victory. Using all the courage I can muster, I tickle him. His 6'2" structure comes crumbling to the ground as he lets out a panicked stream of laughter. He tries to wiggle away from me, but I won't let him. He calls out for help. Markus, who I forgot existed this entire time, tackles me off his friend and traps my arms at my head. I look him over for a moment, this being the first time I've seen more than the back of his head. He's swoon-worthy, reminding me of those

Hollywood stars who model for Calvin Klein. I slightly blush as he keeps my arms pinned and repositions himself. My victim is now a mess, covered in grass and dirt. His face has an evil look as he begins his revenge on me. I squirm and squeal, trying to kick him away.

"Say you're sorry!"

I let out a frantic "never," but I can only take about 30 seconds of the torture before I'm begging for forgiveness. He stops and falls beside me, Markus falls to my other side, and we just laugh and enjoy the moment for all its worth. Within the last month, I've almost forgotten how to laugh. It feels amazing after so long, and I smile to myself.

After dusting ourselves off, we all pile back into the truck. Markus joins us in the cab, and I show them my small find. We snack and I learn things about them little by little. They've been friends for years and went to high school together. We mostly talk about the past to keep spirits high. Jack and Owen see a sign along the road that reads simply: *Now Entering Hagerstown, Maryland*. They give each other a look that I can't decipher. Getting off the main road, a long stretch of road greets us with nothing around except for houses and back roads. I look out into the forest surrounding us. Turning around, I nudge Markus. "Do you know what month it is?"

He sits for a moment, but Owen answers, "November." I nod in acknowledgement, not paying attention to the mood drop inside the cab. They slowly pull off to the side of the road right before a gas station, the first one I've seen in miles. Jack turns around in his seat and takes a deep breath.

"To get where we need to go, we've got to go straight through downtown. I don't really know what to expect." I look at their faces and they are grim.

"Can we not go around?" He shakes his head and explains it will take too much time and the territory is unknown. Taking a moment to prepare, we grab our bags and weapons out of the back. Doing as I'm told, I put everything on, ready to bolt if needed. This causes me to worry. Markus can sense this, I'm guessing, and he places his hand on mine and squeezes, giving me a hopeful look.

We pull away from the side of the road, taking our time, trying to be cautious of what's coming and the unknown that is awaiting us. The air outside has a sharp bite to it. The smell is dull but strong. We make our way down the road and the town slowly comes into view. They knocked the first red light over with a car right at the bottom; the front crumpled into itself. A red film soaks the windshield. Trash and belongings litter the sidewalk. Red splotches are everywhere, soaking the concrete. We pull onto the sidewalk to drive around a multiple car pileup. Decorations for Halloween are up, some knocked loose from neglect. The street is a single road, one way in and one way out. A fountain sits, the water no longer flowing, and I can only imagine how bad the pond below looks. We go over the grass that once was a park most likely bustling with life, saying a tiny prayer as we continue. We pass by city hall and things only get worse.

Storefront windows are busted out, trash cans have been turned over, paper trash and bodies litter the way, cars sit collecting dust.

We stop. In the middle of the only road we can access is a massacre. Bodies line the road in various stages of decay. The smell finds its way into the vehicle and my stomach swirls. The nameless—and some faceless—lay with their insides open to the world around them. Crows and vultures take their part in the circle of life, feasting on the display in front of us. Looking around, we don't see any signs of biters. We jump out cautiously, one by one, and investigate. I head over to an alley and peer in, looking for anything useful. The boys walk forward, weighing their options before deciding to start pulling corpses to the side, making room for us to get through. I peer into the dark entryway, and I see a shadow run by into an open door. I pull off my bow and load it while I approach. Left, then right, I scan every few steps, making sure nothing jumps out at me. I get halfway down when Owen calls for me to come back. I hesitate. My stomach tells me danger is near, but I brush it off as nerves. I scan once more before slowly relaxing my bow and turning to walk away.

Paper crunches under my boot and I see the light coming into view. Getting close to the entrance, I see the boys looking at me. I blush in response to their gazes. Then their faces twist in horror, and I question them with a look of my own, only to be answered by a cold metal object placed to my throat and an arm wrapped around my shoulders, forcing me back into a hard chest. I go rigid as the situation comes to life The unknown figure smells awful, but I can't see them. A male voice reaches my ears in a soft but harsh whisper. "Drop the bow and kick it away or this will be over quickly." My hand releases my bow and I cringe at the weapon clashing on the ground. As soon as the bow hits the ground, the assailant kicks it to the side and away.

"Nobody moves or goes for the bow. Otherwise blondie here is going to need a facelift." The man presses the knife against my cheek and my spine goes rigid.

Owen looks at me and the stranger, trying to come up with a plan. I take this opportunity to speak to the man. "Listen, no one needs to get hurt." I'm trying to sound confident and not like I'm about to need a new pair of pants, which I might add I deserve an award for. He pushes out a laugh that sounds fake and cold.

"Yeah, same as you. Maybe if you play nicely enough, I won't do as much to you as the last one."

My blood runs cold. Questions swarm in my mind as I think about what he could mean. I mutter an "okay," trying to figure out a way to get out alive. Six more men appear wearing bandanas as masks; they don't have actual weapons, more makeshift and found items. One has a long chain draped on both hands that wraps around his arm, another is armed with a bat he's driven nails into, making it more lethal, I guess. The weapons comprise things you can find at a hardware store. I take a shaky breath and move with him. The tiniest ounce of resistance makes the knife dig a little deeper. "Now I'm going to tell you how this is going to go. You can let us keep the girl or we can have your truck. You only get one."

Silence fills the air and I feel everything as he leans down and takes a large breath beside my face. I try to move as far away as possible, but the cold metal presses against my throat, making me wince. The men behind the boys laugh aloud. "How do we know you won't take the truck and her?" Jack asks the man with an icy stare. The man shrugs his shoulders.

"You don't."

I know I just met these guys, but they wouldn't really give me away just like that, right? Oh God, they don't even know me enough to care. Panic shows on my face and in my body. I can hear the wicked grin on his face as he chuckles. Owen takes the keys out of his pocket and slides them across the ground. My heart is racing. He walks us over to where they are, shoving me away from him. I fall to the ground, scraping my hands up. Owen and Jacob run to help me up.

Before we notice, they all run into different areas, leaving the truck. The locking sound was heard, and Markus cursed. "That's how they do it. Lock us out so we have to hot wire it, and breaking into it will send every biter for a mile straight to us."

We look over at the truck and I speak up. "Let's make them regret fucking with us." They look at me like I'm an idiot. Like we should cut our losses and leave. But I don't care. I pull off my bag and remove the plastic pouch that contains the cigarettes and lighters. I pack the cardboard box against my palm and open it, removing one of the tightly clustered cigarettes.

I place the paper filter between my lips, light it, and take a deep inhale. I enjoy the instant hit of the addictive chemical as it makes me slightly lightheaded. With it now lit and hanging loosely on my lips, I shove the plastic bag back into my backpack before zipping it and throwing it over my shoulder. I take another long inhale.

Markus is the first one to connect the dots. "You're a crazy genius." A wicked smile appears on his face, and I grin. His smile makes my heart flutter for some odd reason. I offer him the now burning item. It rests peacefully between two of my fingers. He accepts my offer, using it himself. He holds it for a second and closes his eyes. I admire his attractive features as he passes it back to me. He walks to the truck, lifting himself up into the bed. He makes quick work of the challenge and kicks, sending one of the many cans toppling over. As it spills all along the bed, the fumes hit our noses and I feel a glint show in my eyes.

After joining us back where we stand on the road, I take one last drag before flicking it. As soon as the item leaves my hand, we all take off running like bats straight out of hell. Grabbing my bow off the ground as we pass, I stumble slightly. Jack grabs my pack and drags me along, not letting me lose my balance. Within seconds, it engulfs the truck in flames, and we push ourselves harder to get out of this town. A minute goes by before I hear a loud deadly explosion, and it shakes the ground beneath us. A beacon to all the dead things and a middle finger to the prick who grabbed me. He needed a shower. Luckily, this one is a little too hot for him to survive. When the truck finally gives in to the flames, the surrounding buildings become engulfed in fire. Debris covers the area and affects everything it touches. We just keep going.

I scream a few select words over my shoulder as we leave the main strip. All four of them laugh and hoot, never slowing down.

After a while, when our safety is guaranteed, we slow down to a walking pace. Jack now calls me "Firefly," and Owen has made me jump onto his back as he prances around dancing like a child. "I knew it was a good choice to kidnap you!"

We all laugh and cringe at the same time at the poor choice of words. Despite my many attempts to reason with him, Owen refuses to let me down. After a while, I enjoy the ride. We pass by gas stations along the road and the sun sets. We follow the road, not sure of where we are heading, Jack mentions something about finding a place for the night. Seeing a neighborhood coming into view, we continue our march in hopes of a safe place to rest. Passing the first couple houses, Owen sets me down and I pout slightly.

Enjoying the break from walking has me slightly spoiled. We approach an old colonial-style house make our way up the porch. Taking the time to listen for a moment with the opportunity presenting itself, I load my bow, ready for whatever might pop out at us as we enter the unknown territory. Jacob knocks; easy enough not to echo, but loud enough to be heard inside. We hear one groan, then share looks between ourselves and quietly decide it's worth it. Markus clears his throat to grab our attention, and his head makes a movement toward my weapon with a silent agreement between us all. I nod back at Markus, hopefully understanding the plan as he believes I do.

Jacob goes to the door, checking to see if it's unlocked, and to our surprise, it is. Twisting the handle, he counts down on his fingers from three... I load an arrow and take a breath, steadying my heart. Two... I pull back on the string and line up a shot at where an average-sized adult would stand. One... He pulls open the door. A biter who was once female is right in the doorway. She turns to the entryway, and before it can register in my brain I let the string go. My arrow flies and penetrates right through her mouth, causing the biter to stumble back, but that small stumble was all Jack needed to slam a weapon into her skull. The weapon gets lodged where it connected and it goes down with the corpse as she falls to the floor without making a sound. Taking a second, he pulls the hatchet out of the monster's head. I reload another arrow. We step over her body and file in behind Jack. Somehow we've broken off into two groups. Markus and Owen go to the left, and Jack, Jacob, and I check the right side. We meet in the middle of the kitchen, and I stare at the staircase that needs to be explored.

We make our way up the stairs, each one creaking under our combined weight. We enter a hallway that has six doors; I go to the far room, waiting for my turn to explore. Jacob is first up; he opens the door with his pistol at the ready and ensures his room is infected-free. Owen does the same, walking into a bathroom. I can hear him gag at what I assume is his findings. Jack opens the door to reveal a linen closet and we snicker at him. He walks to the next door to find it empty. He walks back out and nods at me. Opening the door, keeping an arrow at the ready, I enter the room.

Looking around, it resembles a child's room. Dust has settled, but the bright green with blue keeps it bright, minor figures of cars big and small line the shelves. There are picture books and stuffed animals decorating the space, the comforter is a racecar, and walking over to the closet, small clothes hang neatly. My heart aches at the thought. The carpet has a small town with winding roads decorating the place. I see a second door and walk over to it. Opening the door, I notice it's a bathroom that joins the room next door. Flies are everywhere and a horrible stench hits me. I gag as the smell hits my nose, taking my sleeve into my hand and covering my mouth. A strained moan fills the room and I look around, trying to find the source. A curtain covers the tub with a pattern I can't make out in the ill lit place. I walk over to it and snap the curtain open. The shuttering of mental hangers echoes quickly. The sight before me causes a scream to break out in me.

I throw myself back. A small boy, no older than nine, only skin and bones is laying in the tub. His shirt is gone, and his skin looks gray almost. His eyes are too big for his head as they seem to bulge out from their sockets.

His milky hollow eyes frighten me. The biter is so weak that as it reaches me, the movements are slow. It tries to come after me, but stumbles out of the tub headfirst and falls. He hits it at an odd angle, making it lopsided with a sickening crack as what I assume is its neck breaks.

His neck can no longer support the weight of his head, which has it falling to the right, resting right above its shoulder. I crawl backward at the horrific sight. It's barely able to move toward me as it attempts to follow. Markus finally comes running in, asking me what's taking me so long. He stops right behind me and stares at what used to be a little boy trying to claw its way to me. Its hard bites rip through the air in anticipation; a snapping noise rings out as its teeth pang together. Markus grabs my shirt collar, pulling me back, and quickly closes the door. He falls against the wall as reality hits. Tears run out of his eyes, as they did mine, at the godawful sight.

The guys rush in, demanding to know what happened. Markus can't form the words, even though he's trying; only air escapes his lips as we sit there next to the door. I somehow find my voice. "I– I'm guessing that was his mother downstairs. He was in the bathroom." That's all they need as they look around the room. We all knew, but no one wanted to acknowledge the possibility that children could survive the bite.

# Chapter 6

## Unexpected Comforts

Jack took care of the child and buried it out in the yard with what we can only assume is its mother. We all sit in quiet as we take in the appeal of the once-vibrant looking home. The kitchen is still well-stocked, and we devour what we can, packing what we can carry when we leave into our bags. We take some time to explore the house, but I stop fast after all the photos show what those things once were: a happy mother and son. The father is present in all the photos, but we find no signs of him.

Before heading up the stairs, Markus and Jack make sure all the doors and windows are locked. I make the executive decision of choosing the primary suite to settle into for the night. Large paintings cover the walls, complemented by an elegant bedspread that sits neatly made. There are at least ten pillows on this bed, eight of which are decorative with itchy gold thread. The large king mattress sits in the center of the room; the bed frame matches the dresser and side tables. We are all camped out on the carpet, snacking and chitchatting, attempting to wind down enough to soon go to sleep. An old camping lantern sits in the center of our group. The curtains are closed so that hopefully no one can see us. Jacob says something about needing to take a piss and leaves the room, going God knows where. The tone goes soft, and I glance over at the door to the closet, curiosity piquing my interest.

Grabbing my flashlight out of my pack, I flick it on and enter the room, placing the light on one shelf. It gives some visibility, but darkness still shrouds the corners. Running my fingertips over the tops of the fabrics, I stop at a shiny red material. Taking the hanger, I pull out a long satin dress and stare. In the old world, I would have drooled over this, but now I just think about the impracticality of it. Before all of this, this would have been something I'd love to own, but now, with survival being the only thing on my mind most of the day, I can't help but scoff slightly. I place the dress over where it would fit.

The dress would fit beautifully on whoever wore it. I place the hanger back where I found it and open one of the many drawers that line the walls. I find one labeled pants, and I pull it open. Picking up a pair of jeans, the material is light, and the buttons line up to a high waist.

The material is thick but soft, showing they wore it many times with much love. My fingers skim over the front of the jeans, looking them over. My hips are wider than my waist, but I must try, considering the material has some stretch to it. I pull off my old dingy pants, kicking them to the side, and they land in a heap. I put my legs in one at a time and pull them on. I jump a little to get them past my butt, but once I do, they fit rather nicely. Closing the buttons, I smile at my reflection. They highlight my curves in the best way. I turn around and check out my backside and damn, I look good, despite the whole end of world thing going on around us.

After finding a belt that looks like a throwback from the 90s, I smile. Fashion trends do always come back around. I tighten it at my waist snuggly and do some lunges, making sure they will do the job. Satisfied, I moved over to her lingerie, looking at the choice of fancy bras. Stripping off my shirt, I didn't realize how heavy it sat with dirt. My fingers skim along them and choose a random one, gathering the item in my hands.

I hold it to my chest, looking in the mirror. Behind my reflection, I see Markus leaned up against the door frame, his eyes searching my body. I go deathly still, my face a bright shade of red. Our eyes lock and it's become apparent to me I'm not wearing a shirt. I drop the garment and clutch my chest, using my arms to cover myself. He walks slowly toward me. I watch in the mirror as his body exudes confidence in every movement, standing behind me with only enough space that I can't feel his body, but the heat coming off him warms my back. He takes my hair into his hands before moving it all to one side. I shudder at the lightness in his touch.

He leans forward, placing soft, light kisses along the back of my neck. This simple action causes a small moan to escape my lips as he goes across my shoulder. Placing his hands on my hips, he moves me to face him. He cups my cheek in his large, callused hand. We exchange a thousand words with only a look. His face lowers to my height. As he kisses me, his touch is soft and filled with tenderness. I nip at his lower lip, and he opens his mouth for me, allowing me to take the next step. We fight for dominance over the slow kiss. Our lips move as one as the dance for dominance runs its course. Passion slowly builds with every moment, every tug, every stroke.

I pull at his shirt, separating for only mere seconds as he rips it off. My hands explore his chest and stomach, finding a deliciously fit man standing before me. I drop it to the floor. Taking another moment, I take him in. He has strong abs, yes, but the thing that has my stomach flipping is the path that is defined leading right to where I want to be.

My hands clasp around his belt with anticipation as I quickly undo the layer between me and him. He holds my hands still as soon as they release the buckle. He crouches before me, shoving my shoulder back. My body follows the silent command. I lay there on my elbows, watching his cold stare. Excitement flashes in his eyes before looking down. He pulls the belt out of place on my jeans before undoing every button painfully slowly. My heart races as I watch his every move. He pulls at the waist, getting them down past my hips. They get caught, and he kneels in front of me. Little by little, he drags them down, along with my underwear. Throwing them to the side, he takes in a deep inhale. It almost sounds painful as he takes all of me in. He slowly inches up my body, getting right into my ear. His whisper is deep and erotic: "I won't stop until I get to hear you whimper my name." I shiver in delight.

My attitude is gone, and instead I'm completely at his mercy. He bites and nips at my collarbone, down to my breasts, where he takes time with each one, sucking and playing with them. His fingers roll my sensitive buds and tingles shoot down my back just to collect in my stomach. My back arches at the feeling. I let out a labored breath and soft mews. He moves down my stomach, getting right where my hips meet my thigh.

I let out a jump as he kisses in the perfect spot, so sensitive my body attempts to pull away from him, but he takes my hips into his hands and holds me still. His eyes look up to mine and he slowly licks up toward my stomach. The slow drag has me gripping at the air beside me. He takes his time making his way back down, finding the most sensitive areas. He explores each one, trying out different methods, watching my reaction. He widens my legs and I blush from embarrassment.

His voice comes out husky and deep. "Are you ready?" I nod my head, refusing to look at him. His stare alone is sending me to the edge. He takes his hand and starts rubbing my center. I arch with every movement. He takes my face into his other hand, slightly pinching my cheeks together, forcing me to look at him, his eyes dark and powerful.

"I asked you a question and I expect an answer, Firefly."

I let out a yelp while I try to form the words I need. I gasp at air as his pace grows, my hips buck into his hands. The "yes" comes out needy and desperate for more. His approval of my answer shows as he works his way back down, never taking the pressure away from my needy core.

He licks slowly at my bundle of nerves and a shock goes through me as I let out a breathy "yes." He dives right into my soaking core, taking his time, slowly building the speed. My toes curl. The excitement alone is sending sparks through my very being as I'm getting close to the top; my eyes roll back. They never have.

I grip at the soft carpet, trying to keep myself on earth. I try to speak  but nothing makes sense as I can't gather enough air to push any kind of words out, but I still attempt to beg, never wanting him to stop. My entire body gets tense, and the buildup is about to explode.

Just before I'm able to finish, he pulls away. I look at him; betrayal covers my face, but just as our eyes connect, he slams his hardened member inside of me. I bolt upward, a whimper combined with a gasp consumes me. With a loud roar he grips onto the back of my neck as another grips back, securing me where I am. The closeness sends sparks all over my body and I cling to him as he rams deep into me, faster and faster. I claw at his back, trying to keep myself quiet. I curse at the pleasure rushing through me. My entire body screams out.

"Come with me" is all he says, and I pull apart at the seams. With his last stroke out and in, he muffles out a moan and I grip tightly to him. My whimper is combined with his name. He finishes inside of me. Pumping a few more times, he kisses me passionately, never letting go. We stare at each other for a moment before he pulls out, kissing my forehead, calling me by my nickname. Firefly. We lay there for a moment, enjoying the comfort of forgetting the world. I lift myself up and stare at him. He smirks at me and pushes my unruly hair behind my ear.

Stealing one more kiss, he stands and goes through the men's side of the closet, pulling out jeans and a long sleeve black shirt. Grabbing a thick flannel, he pulls on his boots, winks at me, and walks out. I make quick work of dressing myself in new underwear, my newfound pants, and a gray long sleeve that fits to my curves. I pull my hair into a ponytail quickly, but making sure it looks good. Adding to the look, I take out two pieces to frame my face. Grabbing a new pair of socks, I find my field jacket, making sure it fits. I can't help but feel like its fate throwing it on. I enter the bedroom and my face heats. They all look at me with a knowing twinkle in their eyes. Markus sits comfortably in an armchair, his legs wide in a power position, holding his chin in his firm hand, and he smiles at me.

His face shows his movement as he looks me up and down, leaving no room for questions. I blush, lowering my face. I quickly jump into bed, pulling off my boots. I climb into the sheets and my head lands on the pillow. I quickly fall asleep, most likely because of the intense "workout" I was just involved in.

I'm woken up by movement in the bed. I sit up looking around, the sleep still heavy in my eyes. Markus, Jack, and Owen have all climbed into the bed, and I'm in the center, Markus to my right. His arm hugs me and he aggressively pulls me into his chest. Jack has his face to me on my left. I raise my head slightly to my left; Owen is sprawled out snoring. I giggle at myself and see Jacob sitting in the chair, looking out the window. He looks at me and nods, and I return it before laying my head back down, returning to sleep.

# Chapter 7

## The Morning After

Waking up, I roll over and end up on top of someone. I rub my face into their shirt in my mindless sleep haze. I give no thought to who it could be. I feel arms going around my waist, hands slowly traveling down toward my butt. A soft moan leaves my lips and I feel something hard on my stomach. I sit up, rubbing my eyes with the back of my hand. My vision clears only for me to come eye to eye with a handsome, scheming devil: Jack. He has a smirk plastered on his lips; in a deep morning voice, he speaks. "Well, good morning, beautiful." I throw myself backward with a weird yell, not realizing I was so close to the bed's edge.

I roll off and into the floor, legs go flying in a very ungraceful manner. My body contacts a loud thud on the hard floor. Markus and Owen wake up, looking around. Questions ring out above me as I lay with my feet in the air on my back. Their heads pop out from the edge, both looking like puppies as they cock their heads to the side, questioning all my life choices. Jack is laughing so hard he has tears coming from the corners of his eyes. I grumble to myself before slinging my legs, sending myself tumbling onto my butt. They question Jack about what's so funny, and he can't make out anything that makes sense. I grab a shoe and throw it at him and, to my surprise, he dodges it gracefully for whatever time it is. He throws himself off the bed at me and we land with a thump. I begin fake dying, trying to crawl out from under him.

"Why, why is it so bright?"

"Why must I die by walrus?!" I fake yell, adding a dramatic performance. His laughter grows, and so does my smile. Remembering his weakness, I go to attack his sides and he pins my arms back down. Jacob clears his throat at the doorway, and we all jerk our heads at him in sequence.

"We should probably eat and head out, we have a long way to go." The boys grumble, gathering their things to head downstairs. Jack stays just as he is, studying me for a moment. He shoves off his arms and stands, offering me his hand. I accept, and he pulls me up with so much force I land flush against his chest. My hand rests on his shoulder where I latched onto him with the sudden movement, with my other still cradled in his. We both step back nervously. After getting in our shoes, the boys grab some fresh clothes and we head downstairs, where Jacob is giggling like a deranged child. He's sitting beside our stuff with a guitar in his hands. The case rests open at his feet.

"You okay, dude?" I'm slightly concerned about that laugh.

"Yeah, I'm taking this with us."

We don't say a word to him, happy he found something to be excited about. We grab whatever we can to eat from the house, saving our stockpile for the road. After we finish, we load up and look around for anything else useful.

We walk out and head back toward the highway. Light chatter fills the air.

"It's going to snow soon," Jack says as he looks up. We all feel the bite in the air, but that's not a good thing anymore. Snow means survival is only going to get harder, and how things are going, we need no more odds stacked against us.

Our chatter dies down after the crunch of pavement begins sounding under our boots. The roadways are oddly clear; we discuss trying to find another vehicle. It shouldn't be too hard, the only issue being not being able to hot wire. Of course, I vote openly that if we need, Jack should be the one who tries if it comes down to it.

Hours pass by, and every car we stop at is crashed or lodged in some kind of congested area. The bodies just keep piling up, feeling never-ending as we cover more and more ground, and it's getting depressing. As we approach another clogged area, we decide to look and see if any of them can be used. As we look over the cluster of vehicles, I see a truck that seems to be fairly new.

I pass the guys, making it my next target. We've split up to cover more area in our newfound struggle. After reaching the vehicle, I make quick work of lifting the hood. I look for the security sensor. After staring for a hard moment, I finally find the wires and pull it out, disconnecting it from the power supply. Clapping my hands to remove the dust that's created a thick layer over the otherwise shiny vehicle, I walk to the driver's side door and, to my surprise, it opens with a subtle click. I open the door only to stumble back. There's a slouched man in his late forties, by the look of it, on the wheel. Dried blood covers the passenger seat, and down beside the seat is a pistol. I take in the gravesite: putting the two together, I see he shot himself.

I take the pistol and check the clip. Only missing one round. I tuck it into my pants and close the door. Quick feet run behind me, and I freeze. Slowly turning on my heels, I come face to face with a puppy no older than a couple months. The animal is low to the ground, head turned slightly, looking at me, almost expecting me to react a certain way, its tail in between its legs.

It looks like a German Shepherd. I lower myself to the ground and extend my hand to it, praying to myself that this tiny baby has had all its shots and doesn't bite me. The last thing I need is rabies. "Hey, baby, what are you doing out here?" I softly say. The tiny furball sniffs my hand, its ears perk up, and almost like it just remembered how, it jumps all over me. I smile as I pet the pup.

Petting the tiny animal, I feel around its neck and find a cloth-like material, a tag of sorts. I inspecting it. The name reads Tank in clear bold letters. I smile and start talking to the dog. I stand up after placing my new friend on the ground. I take in everything around me before my eyes settle on the bed of the truck. Peeking my head over, I see there's climbing gear in the back, a full body harness, some thick rope, a chain, and a chainsaw.

I pull out the rope. I grab the amount I need for a good-sized tether and use the chainsaw blade to cut it. I grab one of the harness clips and tie the other end to it. I get down and attach it to the collar. Tying him to my belt, he walks alongside me, reaching the guys who look at my new friend, confused. "Do you think that's smart, Firefly?" Markus asks. I cock my head at him and cross my arms.

I will not be taking no for an answer at this. "He can have part of my portions. He's staying with," I say matter of fact. And that's all that I had to say about my new friend before we started walking again. Sadly, we found nothing of value travelwise. It doesn't take long for Tank to get tired, and I put him into my backpack, giggling to myself about it as his head lolls to the side with every sway of the pack.

I'm proud of my finding, and we continue down the road, looking for a vehicle that's not dead, covered in guts, has a flat, or is out of gas. Getting off another exit, we see two gas stations, some restaurants, and an inn. We decide that we've walked enough and head toward the inn. It only has about ten rooms, so the smartest decision is to all pile into one.

We approach the front office and try to find a key; it's trashed, broken vending machines and furniture scattered all around. It's dark inside, so we use our light as we look for something useful. I see a housekeeping cart and notice a plastic card with masking tape on it. "Master key" is scribbled in marker, and I pocket it. Walking out of the office, I go to the first room and try it. It clicks green, and as I go to turn the handle, something slams against the metal door before I jump back. Tank whimpers behind me, ears down.

Pulling him out of my pack, I let him prance around next to me. I walk to a room two doors down and Tank whimpers again, trying to back away. I knock on the door, and I hear another slam farther into the room. I watch him as we walk from room to room, using his reaction to decide which one to open. 107 is the one he seems fine with.

I knock and listen. After a moment, I use the key, the green light blinks three times, and I push open the door slowly. Two queen mattresses are against the wall, so I enter the room and scan the entire place. The bathroom is to the back, and I hope the water is running. The guys join me shortly after and we get comfortable settling into our spots for the night. Tank has claimed one bed, his tail going a thousand miles a minute. I dig the beef jerky out of my pack, and we take turns getting a piece.

"You know, pet stores might not have been raided." The guys look at me and a weird tone settles in the room. "Are you guys okay?" I ask, not enjoying this feeling in the slightest. Markus avoids eye contact with me, and Jack clears his throat.

"We need to decide if it's worth going to the fort, Scarlet. We think it's best if we find somewhere to stay for a while. There's no telling if that base is safe." My face falls. They knew I wanted to go there to see if my friends got the same news as me. Or maybe just within the area. I doubt it. I know Ralph would hope the same if he heard anything similar. But if it's not there, that area will be swarming.

"And you guys already decided?" My voice is low, and they all nod. I throw myself back into the bed. "Well then, I guess we should get some sleep." I turn away from them and I feel Tank curl into a tiny ball beside me. I understand the reasoning behind it, but it doesn't make it hurt any less.

Grabbing our supplies and Tank, we talk about tracking down an animal supply store. He trots beside me; his movements bring me joy all in their own way.

We talk about where a good place to stay for a while would be. We go over motels, farms, hardware stores, somewhere we could make safe. We all go quiet when Tank whimpers. Looking around the area, we see nothing. Tank stares at the trees to our right. Pulling my bow out, I load an arrow, prepared for the worst. Slowly approaching, we hear a strange intake of breath, almost like a wheeze. A sudden joint behind the tree makes us stop cold. Markus picks up a rock and chucks it at the source of the noise, causing a biter to jump back, its movements frantic. It stays crouched to the ground, its back slumped forward, reminding me of a monkey. Letting out a bone-chilling scream, it runs at our group. I aim my bow and let the arrow fly. The creature's frantic and erratic movements cause the arrow to fly right past and misses its target.

Panic feathers in my gut. The ones from before never did that. A shot rings out and it falls, sliding against the ground, stopping right at my feet. I look to see Jacob with a pistol in his hand.

"What. The. Fuck?"

"That one didn't act like the others." Markus grabs a stick and uses it to flip over the monstrosity.

"It's like it was hiding behind the tree, waiting to attack us from behind."

"They aren't smart like that. They just scream and go berserk, almost like a pack mentality," Owen says, his face curling up in disgust.

"What if personalities have something to do with it?" Jacob says quietly. Our heads snap from the creature to him, wanting him to explain himself.

"You know, everyone is wired differently, but certain personalities are more common than others. This could have been some creep. But the ones we've seen before are just common personality types."

Jack scoffs. "So what are we going to see, a biter picking daisies soon?"

Jacob rolls his eyes at Jack's comment but continues.

"No, we have baser instincts. We talked about this in my debate class. We all have a baseline, but certain chemical imbalances affect the mind, depression, perversion. They make up who we are. So, if this sickness takes hold of the body, what if the individual chemicals make them act a certain way?"

We stare at him in shock, me simply because I didn't take him for a debate kid, and everyone else for their own reason.

But it makes sense.

After making sure no more were around stalking us, we continue down the road, talking about different ways of life, wondering if it's just us or another country. We talk about going up to Canada. We know we'll have to live off the grid, maybe take up wax making if that's even possible.

After a while, we just decide to see what we stumble upon and go from there. Owen thinks a larger house so we all have our own rooms would be nice. And whether we need to make a fence. I vote for a fence. After a while, Tank gets tired, and I put him back into my pack. The temperature drops the more distance we cover, and I know I don't want to be homeless when the snow starts. We make it to some back road, and in the distance I see a brick house.

"Maybe we should stop for the night up ahead." The guys look where I'm pointing and agree. Making our way down the long gravel drive, stones crunch beneath our feet. Large trees line the road as we make it to the entrance. The door has an old knocker. Pulling it up, I knock three times and step back. We listen for a moment and I hear no sounds. Opening the door, ready for a fight, we look around the house as untouched dust floats in the air. It has an older style. Dead flowers sit in the entryway on a dark wood table. Scanning the area inside, we find nothing alive, so we continue our search one by one as we investigate the different rooms. They are all generic. The primary bedroom has a fireplace, a large four post bed, and art placed all around. The people who lived here had money, is my guess. I put my bag on the bed and Tank slowly stretches out. I smiled at his cute yawn.

We make our way back to the main floor and discover a basement door. I decide it's better to check it out than ignore it. I open the door and head down, Tank right on my heels. What I see makes me confused.

There are sleeping bags strung around the room, cans are open, and there is a lantern sitting in the middle. I crouch down and pick up a can. It hasn't dried out, so I can only guess someone is here or will be back soon. I hear a shotgun being pumped. Tank crouches and growls. I turn around in my squat position, facing the origin of the menacing noise. A man stands there, rough and hardened from years of stress and work. His gruff has grown and his icy glare hits down to my soul. I clear my throat before speaking. "Listen, I don't want any trouble. I was only trying to find shelter before the storm hit. I'll just leave."

His eyes stay trained on me, ignoring Tank. "Is it just you?" is all he says. Hopefully, he'll be less likely to kill me if I tell the truth.

"No, I'm in a group with four other people. We just got out of a city to the east, and we are exhausted." Deciding to tell the truth seems to be the right choice.

He looks at me, raising his eyebrow, and approaches me. He tells me to drop my bow and kick it over to him. I do since I want to live. He picks it up and puts it around his arm. "I want to see your buddies, and if all goes well, I'll give this back."

I nod at him and let out a yell. "Hey, guys, there's someone in here." I hear footsteps running toward me and they stop at the threshold, looking at the scene. My arms are raised in a surrender position and my mouth opens before my brain can stop it. "Can I just say always being the hostage sucks ass?" The man holding the gun laughs out loud for a minute. We just look at him. My arms stay as they were.

"How many times have you held a girl hostage?" The Unknown Man asks his face making a weird expression

I shrug my shoulders as i answer , "Twice that I know of, but weird stuff happens in this world." They all choke out a laugh. I feel my cheeks get heated.

Jack looks at me with a smile and says, "well be sure to let any kidnappers in the future know It's our turn to be held hostage." They make jokes about setting up a meeting.

The man lowers his gun and shakes his head. "Well, I see your group is alright, but I can't say whether you can hide out here with us. It's not just my decision." We look over at him, confused. He stomps his feet six times in a row. In a couple minutes, six people come out of the damn woodwork. Three girls, two boys, and an older woman. The kids look to range from 10 to 17. They all stand behind the man. "What do y'all think? Should we let them stay for a few days, or throw them into the storm?"

The youngest girl peeks out from behind his legs and her eyes light up when she sees Tank. "Puppy!" is all she says. She runs to Tank and starts loving him, calling him a good boy.

Me and the man look at each other and I shrug at him with a small smile before watching the girl play with Tank again. He lets out a sigh and says, "Well, well, I guess Rose decided for everyone then. The people with the puppy get to stay."

The storm hit shortly after. We all huddle together to keep warm, Tank curled up to my right. As the wind pounds against the house and the storm wages war against the brick, I quickly fall asleep.

# Chapter 8

## Why Does Everything Change?

When we wake back up, the storm has settled slightly, and the little girl, Rose, is poking at my cheek. An older girl in her teens stands behind her, looking nervous. I crack open my eyes to look at her. "Yes, darling?" I ask in a hushed tone.

"Can Rose take out the puppy?" the teenage girl asks. I can feel the anxiety in her voice.

I look over at Tank then look back at her. "Not yet, but you can feed him if you'd like."

Rose's head bounces up and down and she runs off somewhere. The older man comes back with her; she's pulling him. I sit up and hold my hands in my lap. He has a cup of something and offers it to me. The cup is warm, and I delight in it. Taking a sip, I recognize the taste of coffee. I hum in joy as I sip away.

"I'm Jason," he says, and he sits down next to me as Rose feeds Tank.

"Scarlet. Thank you for letting us huddle down here till the storm passes through."

He "hmms" in acknowledgment. "My daughter would be proud of the decision. I can only hope." Sadness fills his eyes.

"May I ask, is Rose your grandchild?"

He looks at me, searching my face for something. "They all are my wife's, and I was watching them while their parents went off on a joint business trip. They never came back.

"Tommy and Clarissa are from their mom's first marriage, and Chris and Beth are from their father's first as well. Rosie is their child together, but my daughter and her husband love each child as if they were their own. Tommy and Beth are a handful, but the other kids are angels, all things considered. My wife Laila gave me an earful about extending the offer because of your dog, but Rosie was so happy. All she could talk about was him all night. I had to promise that we would ask you if she could play with him in the morning just for her to lie down." He laughs a little and crow's feet show beside his eyes.

"Listen, all I'm saying is please don't make me regret this. Give me a little faith in humanity again." I nod in acknowledgement.

The boys are still fast asleep, and I stand up, stretching out my limbs. I call Tank to go outside, and he gets up, stretching himself. "Big puppy yawn!" Rose smiles and her little eyes light up. I smile at her. Tank and I make our way to the door and walk outside. He sniffs around the snow, trying to find the perfect spot. I get my bow ready, just in case. He finishes and we walk back inside. There's a fire lit in the living room. I stand at the doorway as Tank trots over to it like he owns the place, and I slowly follow behind. Rose bounds over to Tank and the other kids look at me; their expressions look concerned. Paying no mind to it, I sit beside the fire and bathe in its warmth.

The oldest boy, Tommy, speaks up. "What are you guys planning?" The question sounds hostile.

With a quick shrug, I answer, "Just trying to find somewhere safe. We only have to wait for the storm to finish, then we'll be gone." I never look away from the fire.

"Just watch yourself and that mangy mutt of yours. We don't need you to bring down issues on us." This response sends me into anger quickly. Before I can stop myself, I stand up and turn around, towering over his sitting figure.

"Listen, kid, I will watch myself and my dog, but you don't insult the things I love. Got that?" My tone is harsh when he looks at me. My outburst seems to do the job intended, and I return to the fire. Why did that upset me so much? Tank comes over to me and nuzzles into my side. I pet him. The storm has settled, and I go looking for my men. I see them talking to the old man and I stop. I can hear them, but they can't see me. The hushed whispers are hard to make out, so I decide to just waltz in there with all my glory. I make my way around the corner, and they see me, but to my surprise, they continue their conversation.

"Hey, Firefly," Markus says. "We were just seeing if they'd like to come with us." I nod in acknowledgement, slightly blushing at how he acknowledged me, included me. It's not something I'm entirely used to, and my heart skips half a beat at his actions. He continues, "They have an RV. I think it would help us out a lot."

I stand beside Jack, and I feel a tender touch as I'm pulled down to Markus's lap. He wraps his arms around my torso as they continue the conversation. Jack tenses visibly in the corner of my eye. Turning to him, I send a curious look. He avoids my gaze, and they keep the conversation alive, talking about how our group could help them out. The old man says the only issue he sees is Laila. She's the reason they haven't left yet; she fears the dangers associated with leaving the house. Apparently, she's never even seen one of the infected.

There's a military base close to here where, when radio frequencies were still going, they were calling for all survivors to come and join them. They called themselves the Brothers in Offense, or BIO for short. Jason ends the conversation, saying that he'll speak to his wife tonight, and if all is well, we'll load up as soon as the snow melts.

We help prepare dinner, and tonight we share a meal like some close, happy family. It's weird but oddly comforting; we laugh, and I learn a good bit about the kids.

I finally learn that my men are around the ages of 26 and 27. The boys about crap themselves when I tell them I just turned 21 back in June. We share stories about what the first days were like. I tell them about my original group and about how I got separated. Owen tells the story of them saving me from the horde; I still call it a kidnapping, but it's a matter of opinion I guess. They were all on different sports team and I tell them about how I played softball until I had to quit for reasons I refuse to share.

We answer questions the kids have about the adventures and how we got out alive. The girls ask why the boys call me Firefly instead of Scarlet because my name is so pretty. I blush at their comment, but not a moment later, before we can share the story in a child-friendly way, loud static rings out through the house. The old man tells Tommy to go turn his crap off and he bolts from the room. He doesn't come back for the rest of the night. Apparently, Tommy sleeps upstairs by himself while the girls share a room, but because it feels safer, they normally end up in the cellar. After dinner and all the plates are fully picked over, I end the night early. Tank stays curled up beside Rose as she brushes his fur with a hairbrush. Can't say I blame him; honestly, I'm slightly jealous of the tiny womanizer.

Making my way to where our stuff is, I lay down and make quick work of getting to bed. I throw off my jacket and shirt, wearing only the sports bra underneath. I stare at my reflection in the window. Angry scars stare back at me. The scars show all the years I endured, but I still hate them with everything in my being. My face has gone slim, but my arms are gaining back some weight. All the fresh cuts have healed a dark red. They litter my body. I take off my boots and set them beside me. Maybe I should chop off my hair to give myself a fresh start. Closing my eyes and listening to the surrounding noises, I hear the light static again, but this time, a voice comes through.

I sit up and try to listen. Making my way around the corner, slowly looking around and up the stairs, I see a door cracked open. The light fills the hallway. Curiosity always gets the better of me. As I approach the door, I hear Tommy's voice speaking in silence. "Yes, we are about three hours outside Michigan Lake, there is my family and recently three men and a woman have joined us."

The static cuts out and a man comes through the speaker. "Eleven members of your group. We can send a team out to extract you as soon as the storm clears." Tommy waits a moment before another voice cuts through. This one is different, and it sounds harsh.

"Describe the woman."

Tommy waits for a moment and begins. "Roughly five feet four, wears gray and black clothing, long blonde hair, scars and tattoos on her upper torso. Uses a compound bow as a weapon and has a mutt that follows her around everywhere."

The man responds quickly: "Has she come in contact with any of the infected population?" The voice sounds panicked.

"Yes."

The voice responds with a "Roger."

I hear him scribbling down something as I sneak back down. Returning to my little puddle of blankets, I curl into them. Why would he give up the position of this house? Is he really that shielded from the surrounding chaos? Does he not realize the dangers outside? After struggling with what I've learned, I pull myself up and throw on my shirt. Making my way around the house, I come to find everyone in the living room surrounding the fireplace. I walk up to Jason and ask him to come with me for a moment. He excuses himself from the conversation and we exit the room.

Once we're out of earshot, I inform him about what I heard and apologize for eavesdropping, but it was concerning. I tell him some information about the group we met before, and this look of fury slowly grows on his face.

He yells out Tommy's name before he bounds around the house, up the stairs. I hear the door get kicked open and Laila is yelling at him to calm down. We all run up the stairs, and as we gather, the radio breaks to life: "Confirm the address. 668 Donald Drive, Michigan. Please repeat the city. Over."

Jason's eyes go wide as he looks at his grandson. "What HAVE YOU done, boy?!" He steps back, and the old man seems younger in his rage. "DO YOU NOT REALIZE THE DANGERS OUT THERE?! YOU'VE PUT THE ENTIRE FAMILY AT RISK!"

Tommy shakes his head and tries to explain that they'd be safer with them. Rose clutches to me and I pick her up, rubbing her back, trying to soothe her. I speak up as she clutches into my shirt. "Jason, we need to leave now. Your family is in danger and so is mine. These people out there are gruesome and heartless. The female population has been wiped out and most survivors are men. You've got to see what I'm trying to get at here."

He gets what I'm trying to tell him without scaring the children. He takes a deep breath and turns to his wife. "Pack up anything that's useful for survival. We are all leaving. Tonight." He turns and grabs the radio, raising it over his head. Tommy yells at him to stop, but he throws it on the ground with enough force to shatter the metal box. He stomps it and refuses to look at Tommy. "You've disappointed me, you've put the family in danger. I expected better out of you."

We can feel the heartbreak in the air; the tension is so thick, you could slice it with a knife.

Apparently, Laila is not happy about leaving; at least that's what we gather from her yelling at Jason that he's crazy. Rosie hasn't left my side, and my gut swears something bad is going to happen. But they all get packed up.

We all try to settle ourselves for the journey in the morning. Tank jumps off my lap where he was previously laying and starts exploring, but keeps me within eyesight. Jacob comes into the room with some wood and loads it into the fireplace and stokes the fire, keeping it alive a little longer.

We all sit around the area. Jacob softly plays his guitar, creating a soothing melody. I lay down on the floor, stretching my body out and enjoying the comforting warmth that surrounds me. Owen's giant frame casts a shadow over me as he offers his hand. I raise an eyebrow but go along with it, using it to get up and stand.

"Jacob, add some happiness to that melody, will ya?"

Hand in hand, Owen guides us in a twirling dance across the empty room, bathed in the fire's warm light. The music speeds up and we go in and out, spinning and switching. I'm barely able to keep up, but I feel a smile stretch across my face. By the end, Owen dips down and my leg kicks out. We are both laughing, as are the others at the display before them. I take a big gulp of air and laugh. Tank has moved to the door and paws at it. My head turns toward my fluffy companion, and I excuse myself, figuring he needs to go to the bathroom. I follow him to the front and take him outside, stepping off the porch but keeping close to him. He sniffs around, looking for the perfect spot, as always.

I cross my arms to my stomach, trying to toughen out a little longer in the cold temperature. I hear something move next to us and I turn around, looking for the source. Tank runs in that direction, and I take off after him, whispering, yelling at him to come back. Every worst-case scenario runs through my head as I lose sight of him and pick up my pace. Turning a corner, something slams into my chest, sending me onto my back.

I groan in pain. The snow soaks my jacket and hair as I try to orient myself. A large weight is planted on my stomach, and opening my eyes, I see a man dressed in all black. He has a piercing in his eyebrow and black hair decorated with an unnatural silver at the ends. He slams his hand over my mouth, directing me to be quiet. I nod my head. "I'm going to remove my hand. If you make a single noise, I'm going to kill everyone in that house," he says. I nod my head aggressively, understanding the danger I'm currently in. He removes his hand from my mouth and makes quick work of grabbing my wrists. I fight him for control. I get a good scratch across his face and neck, but the only thing I gain is him getting pissed off and more aggressive with me.

Flipping me over underneath him, I try to crawl away but fail horribly. I claw at the ground, tearing grass and snow off in chunks. The snow bites at my fingertips. He grabs one arm and slams it into my back before securing the other to it with some kind of smooth cord. He gets off me and I use my shoulder to push myself up and run.

I hear him curse and chase after me. I make it to the porch steps and climb, my feet hitting the boards loudly. He catches up with me quickly and throws himself onto me. We land with an *oomph*. I try to make some space by pushing my legs out while on my butt. I call out for help as he slings me over his shoulder as if I weigh nothing at all. He walks away, muttering something under his breath. My cries for help don't stop, and I feel panic in me the farther away we get. I thrash around, kicking and slinging my body around, but he tightens his hold on me.

He heads toward the road and I yell, screaming any kind of noise possible, hoping I'm loud enough to wake anyone— *everyone*—up. The man curses and starts running for the road toward a car. There appears to be someone in the driver's seat. Throwing me into the back, my scream is cut off by the door slamming in my face and I see figures running out of the house. Someone spots us and starts running my way, but the car takes off. The stranger in the driver's seat slams the gas pedal down, causing it to jerk us forward. I wiggle my hands down my butt and get my legs out. I am so tired of this always happening to me; why can't they kidnap Owen, for Christ's sake? I sling myself forward, putting my arms over the headrest, linking them against the driver's throat.

He claws at my arms, trying to get me to let go. I push against the seat to give myself more leverage. The guy who grabbed me takes the wheel and tries to keep us on the road. He pulls at one cord while I'm jerking myself back, trying to break the driver's neck. I fall back, knocking the air out of my lungs. I strain, trying to refill my lungs. The guy who grabbed me crawls into the back with me.

He looks pissed. I scramble as far as I can away from him. He grabs onto my throat and squeezes. I try to claw at his hands and arms. My vision clouds black, and I grab at his face, trying to get him to let go. Unable to get air, my heartbeat rings in my ears. A distant ring sounds out, and in a last-ditch attempt to get him to let go, I go slack. He holds my neck, his grip tightens, and I realize I messed up—possum is not the way to go here. With my final thought echoing in my brain, I feel my eyes flutter and roll back.

# Chapter 9

## Why Is it Always Me?

I shiver awake. The goosebumps on my arms tell me my jacket has been removed. Rubbing my hands down my face, I can't make sense of where I'm at. The room is pitch black and I can't make anything out using my hands. I push off the ground to try to and stand, and my head pounds against itself.

Feeling around, I walk until I contact the icy surface of a wall. Using it to guide me, I take a couple steps and there is a tug at my waist. I use my fingertips to find the item. A light fabric material with some kind of center strip sits snugly at my waist. I pull at it, and I hear a distant clang on the floor. Investigating further, I feel cold metal, and patting down the chain, I find a lock connecting me to it. Looking for some kind of fault in my restraints, I can't find any. I try to pull at the cord; throwing my body weight into the jerking and tugging does nothing but cause friction between my shirt and skin. I continue to try, but all I get in the end is feeling like I have carpet burn.

The light flicks on, showing me a blinding white room. Shelves sit across the room from me, a metal door directly in the center. It looks heavy, and there's a small window with lines going across it.

I hear a beep and I guess that means the lock is released. On the other side of the now-open door is the same man who grabbed me. He stands in the doorway for a few minutes, taunting me with his freedom. I see now he is wearing a black t-shirt and cargo pants with boots.

A utility belt sits on his hips. The items vary from your everyday security job. There's a badge on his chest with the name *Adam*, and the word *Security* sits below it in plain black letters. He walks in, stopping directly in front of me. He stays resting his arms across his chest. He looks familiar, but I can't pinpoint from where. I straighten out my back to seem taller, trying to hide the fear that's blooming inside me. I don't want to show weakness, but in my current state, all I can do is pretend I'm not about to crap my pants.

"Please take a seat." That simple sentence pisses me off. His voice is calm and confident. It comes out smooth, like one would sound at an important meeting. Deciding that all I have left is my pride, I cock my eyebrow at him, challenging his authority. He repeats himself, and I can see my minor act of defiance has pissed him off; as he repeats the words, his teeth clench slightly. When I don't listen to him the second time, he reacts by shoving me to the ground. He puts force behind it; a lot more than necessary, might I add. I fall right on my butt and topple over slightly, rolling onto my hands and knees. I glare at him through my hair. I push myself up to stand once again, not accepting this abuse. and he returns the favor by pushing me over yet again, only this time I land on my back. The force hurts like a bitch, and I clench my teeth, propping myself up with my hands to lean on my elbows.

I stare at him, trying to show no emotions. He crouches in front of me, extending his hand. He pushes some of my hair back behind my ear and out of my face, dragging his knuckles down my face. I pull away. As I turn my head away from his hand, he grips my chin harshly.

"You are a lot of trouble. Hopefully, it's worth it." His eyes are relaxed as he speaks. His tone is not harsh or hateful, but almost disappointed.

"Why?" My voice comes out hoarse from the screaming I did earlier. Tightening his grip on me, "You'll find out." He states this simply like you would in an everyday conversation. Throwing my head to the side like he's discarding a piece of trash, he makes his way behind me and unhooks the chain from the wall. When I hear it hit the ground I take the opportunity presented and fly to my feet, rushing for the door.

I get a couple steps away before I'm jerked back. My back screams in pain at an odd angle and I hit the ground yet again. "God damn it," I say out loud. This is getting annoying. Grabbing onto the chain, he pulls my body back to him and looks down at me. He shows no hint to what he is thinking, and this makes my blood pressure rise. Why can't he be the typical kidnapper and just tell me what the hell is going on?

He walks past me and opens the door with the chain still in his hand. He uses it like a tether of shorts. I'm half-tempted to bark like the bitch he is treating me as, but I decide against it. He might kill me if he thinks I'm that weird. Tugging at the chain and telling me to get up, I comply slowly and follow.

I wouldn't put it past this asshole to just drag me to the destination he has in mind. Once we exit the room, he directs me to go left. As we make our way down, there's not a single window in sight. The concrete walls are freaking me out.

I spot the momentarily saving grace at the end of the hallway: elevators. We both enter. He scans his badge and presses the button for the third floor. The lift hums to life. The ride is short and silent; they could at least have some damn elevator music in this thing. When the door opens, he strolls right past me, expecting me to follow, but I stay still. The door closes, and I grip the railings. He tugs harshly at the chain, and I let out a muffled huff as I latch on harder. The door closes and I quickly push the button to take me to the first floor. The death box goes down, and the chain becomes less slack within seconds, pulling me toward the door.

I scream and try to stay where I'm at. The pulling on my waist is harsh and makes me cry out. This is not what I planned to happen. Why the hell didn't the chain just come with me? Why didn't I rip it out of that bastard's hands before I attempted my great escape?

I smash the stop button and the elevator halts, but to my surprise, instead of staying where it's at, it moves again to the third floor and the door opens. This time, the douchebag is there, and so is another person. He slams the chain back, pulling me with it. Landing on the floor, I try to bolt, but the stranger grabs me by the back of my shirt and throws me against the wall. My face hits the ugly beige wallpaper and bounces off. I feel a trickle of blood escape my nose. I struggle as he presses into my body with his.

Tears fall down my face as I beg them to just let me go. The stranger leans in, I can feel his breath. As he does this, my body gets a shiver of fear at the threat that hangs in the air. Whispering softly, he says, "If you keep struggling, I won't be able to restrain myself." I freeze at that. The threat does not go unnoticed. He speaks into my ear again, only this time calling me a good girl. Disgust rushes down my body and I want to puke. Tightening his grip, he throws me off the wall, making me almost trip over my own feet. I stumble, trying to keep myself up right.

Why are these assholes so rough? I've had enough of this. I turn around and kick Adam—I assume that's his name—right in the family jewels. He drops, letting my chain fall. I quickly gather it up and take off down the hallway, passing doorway after doorway and cutting a corner. I run into a random room and close the door, pressing my body against the door.

I hear them run by, their walkie-talkies blaring. I'm in a hospital room. Looking at the device around my waist, I twist it around. The light inside this room shows me what I need to do, and I make quick work undoing it. It falls to the ground with a thud, and I bolt into action, going over to the window and looking down. There is a rooftop one floor below me.

I take in everything around me and an idea pops into my head. Stripping the bed, I say a tiny prayer, hoping this will actually work. I tie the sheet to the railing and tie them all together. I push the bed against the window. It will take me most of the way there. I try to open the window, pulling and pushing, but as luck would have it, it doesn't budge. Looking over the metal frame, I notice it's screwed shut. Sending a curse out loud, I scan the room. I notice a metal IV pole. Making my way to it, I grab it and unscrew the plastic knob that has the ends that hang the medications.

I jump on the bed and listen for a moment. When I think it's clear, I make a swift, wide swing, throwing everything I have into it. It bounces off and doesn't even cause a crack. I try again and again. Within four hits, I hear them outside the room. I get violent with it, trying to get it to come loose at least.

I lift it over my head to try again as the door slams open. I turn around and there stands Adam, the sicko, and two more people. "Stay the fuck back!" I yell out, raising the pole in a defensive stance.

Adam approaches me slowly. "Drop the weapon," he demands, but I scoff at him.

"Yeah, I will as soon as you fuck off."

I swing the metal pole at him, not noticing someone diving at my ankles. They knock my legs out from under me and I fall on the bed. They drag me to the floor, kicking and screaming.

"Leave me alone, I did nothing to you." I'm trying to reason with them, or maybe myself. "I know nothing and I'm nobody. "

I'm tossed onto my stomach with my arms landing beside my head. Before I can make any sort of move, someone slams their boot onto the hand holding my weapon, I scream out as the pain explodes. I try to pull it away from the owner of the boot, but the man applies more pressure as I continue my struggle. The pain goes from throbbing to blaring. It has a fire of its own, screaming out, and I beg them to stop.

"For the love of God, please," I beg, not ever having known a pain such as this. Tears flow from my eyes, my mouth becomes dry, and I can't stop trying to pull my hand away. I feel like an animal caught in a bear trap. My assailant doesn't move, and I'm just causing myself more pain as I continue to struggle, but I can't stop. After what feels like an eternity of his twisting his foot on my hand, he lifts his boot.

Jerking my hand back, I cradle it into my body, pushing myself against the wall, crying, wailing. The pain is so explosive; I've felt nothing like this before. What kind of cruel monster does this? The ripple and throbbing of it has me biting my lip, drawing blood, but it does nothing to help. Pushing myself back into the wall, wishing I could become one with it, I stare at them wildly. The feeling of a cornered wild animal yet again floods through me, and my heart hammers in my chest.

My breath is quick, and the tears don't stop. My eyes are widening, becoming dry despite the tears. Adam kneels down to my level and harshly grabs the wrist of my injured hand.

I turn with his movements, going wherever he leads me. There is a glint in his eyes as he watches me, a sickening smile, and I'm terrified of what he is about to do. He hovers over my hand and makes a ticking noise as he inspects it. He cradles it in his, slightly covering it, and the heat from his palm makes it even worse. I whimper as he does this. Tears wheel in my eyes, creating a fountain that I can't stop

"See what running does. I thought you'd have been smarter than that."

I kept quiet, whimpering from the pain. I dig my teeth into my lower lip yet again, waiting for the pain he will inflict upon me.

One of the unknown men speaks up. I don't see him, as I'm too focused on this lunatic holding my injured hand. The stranger's voice is soft, almost conquered. "Dom, you need to be careful. We had to travel for hours just to find her. We can't risk losing another one."

My mind races with questions. The only one that makes it out of my mouth is simple. "Where am I?" They ignore my question. The man who told the man I considered as Adam to be careful with me walks over. I try to pull my hand away from Dom and he squeezes it, sending another wave of pain before letting it go. He stays kneeling where he is and watches as I push against the wall.

The stranger squats down to my level and in a soft tone he speaks to me. "Calm down, it's okay." Placing an arm under my knees and behind my back, he picks me up like I weigh nothing. I cradle my hand into myself, trying to stay quiet, but I can't help the whimpers that come out.

They walk me to a different elevator. Silence hangs in the air yet again, but I enjoy it so much more now that the person holding me almost protectively remains calm. He sends a look of concern to me here and there as we make our way up.

After entering his badge into the unit, we walk past different rooms. I look around, trying to figure out what is going to happen. We reach a room labeled 562, and he uses his badge to enter. Instead of doing what I think he's about to do, he doesn't put me down, and I feel grateful for it.

I keep quiet. My hair has fallen into my face, shielding me, as another stranger enters the room. Dressed in the same outfit, he has a syringe in his hand. Panic floods through me and I try to throw myself out of my newfound prison. He drops my legs and latches his arms around my waist. I pull and push, trying to get away. I feel a prick on my shoulder and a burn. I struggle against the behemoth of a man, screaming and throwing my legs out, trying to kick the other in my pursuit of violence.

My eyes feel heavy, and my legs become like Jell-o. I fall back into the man as I go more and more slack. The man who I just failed miserably at assaulting catches me, picking me back up in the same position as before. A question is asked about my hand, and the behemoth tells him Jeremy slammed his foot on it.

The stable douche reaches for my hand as I try to fight the sedation. I swing it at him, knocking his glasses off his face and sending a fresh round of pain through my injury. I use my good hand and pull myself away, fighting as best as I can. I swing out again, slurring my speech. "G-go few yourself." The words make little sense. I question my vocabulary as I slow down and become more sluggish. Everything shuts off and my head hits the man's shoulder.

# Chapter 10

## Return of History

The throbbing in my head becomes more pronounced as I lift it, the sensation of wakefulness slowly taking over. I go to cradle it in my hands, but they hang suspended, unable to complete the motion. I'm awake now, with my eyes open. I'm in a hospital bed. The area is decorated in beige and brown. The large window allows sunlight to fill the room. Clear plastic tubing carries something to my arms. I see a blood bag on one side and on the other side sits another. My head is pounding, and my mouth is dry. I see light blue padding around my wrists; I twist them around and notice my movement is restricted.

I jerk against the restraints. Looking down, I notice I've been changed into a gown; the teal material hangs loosely on me. I struggle and thrash, attempting to break free.

Two men arrive after my yell. I pause and lock eyes with them, wanting answers. "What are you doing to me? Why am I here?"

The person on the right sits at the foot of the bed before starting. He wears glasses and a lab coat. "I'm sorry we must meet in these unsavory conditions. I'm just going to cut straight to the point. There is no way to sugarcoat this. I'm not sure if you're aware of this, but a lot of the female population died in the first couple weeks from sickness. The ages fall between 17 to around 50. We lost most of our staff in that time. The genetic material in much of the female population from years of evolution cannot survive the attack from the virus. As they all came in contact with the airborne spores, their reproductive tracts became too weak and failed.

"If society was still running and operational, it could have been avoided, but due to not receiving proper care, we've chalked it up to sepsis. Because of this, females within this age group are becoming harder and harder to find. But it's been nearly impossible to find a vaccine, or "cure," as some of my men put it. I don't understand why it's only the female population, but I have a feeling the ones who survived are the key to figuring out how to get through this.

"This is where you come in." He opens his arms as a presentation . I stare at him, dumbfounded.

"And this concerns me why?" The anger in me is building and I am so pissed off. I can't catch a damn break.

"Well, let me tell you what we have discovered first!" He has a gleam of excitement in his eyes and it's a little terrifying.

"We started by infusing your blood with that of an infected subject. All in a petri dish, of course. We collected samples of your blood, and upon testing we noticed your cells had a very interesting reaction to those of the infected. Instead of the infected cells taking over your red blood cells, they simply attached. After that, we started micro-infusing you with the infected samples.

"While keeping you hydrated, we slowly increased the sample size. We've kept you sedated to keep a close eye on you, as well as to ensure you wouldn't become a danger to us or yourself. We've been monitoring you closely and—"

I panic, cutting off his long, drawn-out speech about how they signed my death certificate. "You infected me. I'm going to die. I'm going to turn into one of those things." I pull at the restraints. "I've killed to stay alive just for you fuckwits to kill me tied down to a bed!"

My breathing picks up as I continue to scream at them, trying to pull off the restraints.

The man who was standing behind the lunatic rushes over and pushes me down. I snap at him with my teeth. If I'm infected, I'll at least take some of these fuckers out with me. I feel a heaviness in my eyelids, and I look over to see him putting something in my IV line.

My eyes roll back, and I feel a vibration. My body thrashes.

# Chapter 11

## Dominic

Staring at the data in front of me, I feel pride that I'm the one that grabbed her. I'm the one who brought her back to us after so many years.

Her DNA was formed with the infection, simply perfection, just like all those years ago. But instead of completely rewriting like it did in all the failed attempts, it merged, creating something else. We've had many test subjects trying to replicate her, replace her, but she...she's the key.

There's something about her that made her compatible. We never got that far in the past. They were always so careful with her. Scared if she snapped, it would end years of work. But now I'm going to finish the work and she'll finally be my darling yet again. I can't wait to see how these trials go. She's feisty, cunning, even more so than before. The way she fooled us long enough to get away made me feel something I haven't felt in a while. Excitement.

The way she screamed when they broke her hand made me almost lose my composure altogether. That look on her face of terror was everything to me somehow.

When we compared her genetic code with the data from before, I nearly choked on my drink. Who would have thought we would find her after so long?

After we combined her blood with the infected blood supply, she healed rapidly. Her injury healed in two days. I knew we all developed different things through the infection during the trials, but this is so much more. The possibilities are endless with her and I. Strolling down the hallway, I make a point of going to her room every day. Actually, being here is almost too much to bear.

I see John and Steven as I pass the nurse's station outside her room. "What's going on? What happened?"

John looks at me and shakes his head. "She had a seizure like I've never seen. She foamed at the mouth. Her vitals are stable for the most part, but we're in the dark here. Her temperature hasn't changed, but her heart is slow, almost too slow."

I walk to the open door and enter. She's fast asleep. The blankets are pulled off her, and they have released the restraints in case it happens again. I lean down and listen to her breathing; it's steady. Her eyes are moving under her lids rapidly, like she's dreaming. I take a deep breath, calming my nerves in her scent. When she got here after sedating her, I took care to clean her. I spent special time with her, making sure she was kept to the pristine standard her father always needed from her.

Her blonde hair has a natural curl to it, and it's laid out under her head. I stroke the soft strands and feel myself getting hard. I pull my hand away, turning sharply as I walk out.

John walks beside me, telling me we need to give her a couple days before starting the subject trials. I agree and inform him to keep her sedated. She's a smart little one, and I'm not about to lose her. We've found plenty of men, but females are becoming almost impossible to track down. I wouldn't put it past her if we lost her again to disappear forever. We had to travel four hours to find her. But it was so worth it. Her father is going to be over the moon at this discovery, and I will be the one to tell him.

# Chapter 12

## Scarlet

I'm so tired of being knocked unconscious. Lifting my hand, I hold it into view. I raise up and throw my legs over the side, ripping out the IVs. Staring at the window, I see that it's afternoon, and the sun hangs low in the sky. My reflection stares at me and I notice something hanging on my nose. I feel the strange object; it's smooth plastic. I grip onto the unknown device and start pulling it out. The act has me gagging and I want to puke. Finally getting it out, I throw it on the ground, and blood and a strange brown fluid cover the surrounding tiles.

Standing up, I look around slowly. I make it to the door and poke my head out. The hallway is clear. I quickly take the opportunity presented and move to the nurse's station, looking for anything interesting. Opening drawers, I dig through the contents, lifting a binder. I place it on the desk amongst the chaos present. Swiping my hand under a stack of paper, I find something that is hard plastic.

Gripping onto it, I pull it out, inspecting it. I smile at what sits in my hands; a badge. *Chelsea. Nursing.* I clutch the badge in my hand. Racing down the hall, I scan the surroundings, looking for a way out. Footsteps ring in the distance. I see a badge scanner on a random door, and I quickly use the badge to duck into a linen closet.

I press myself into the wall, away from the window. Men pass and I hear them talking about random shit. Pressing my hand over my heart, I count to ten. After the small countdown, I gather my courage and open the door. As I slip back out, I listen to every bump possible, making sure my quiet escape will be a success.

My feet make small noises as they hit the ground. Lifting my heels, I settle on my tiptoes, trying to make them less noticeable. I approach a stairwell door and slip into the corridor. The air is chilly, bone-chilling almost. Emergency lights make the path visible.

I fly down the stairs, picking up speed, ignoring the fact that my butt is on display for anyone to see. 4th floor, 3rd floor, 2nd floor, 1st floor! I see the emergency exit door, and I slam into it. I arrive in a tunnel. I curse myself for not thinking ahead, but I don't really have a plan except to get out, so that's what I'm doing.

I see the last door and I fly into it, preparing for anything, except it's like a brick wall. I bounce off it because of the force I applied. I jiggle the push releases and bang on it. I yell out, not caring about making too much noise. The door is locked up tight. I bang on it in desperation, trying to get it to open. I wail out. My freedom is so close. I put my back against the glass wall and slide down.

I cry out loud. All I wanted was to get out. To die free. Lost at my pity party, I don't hear the footsteps coming down the stairs. I recognize the tune that is being hummed out, but I can't pinpoint it exactly. I look to see Dominic twirling keys in his hand as he continues to hum. He gets to the last step and speaks as he approaches me.

"Did our little guinea pig try to flee the cage? It's a shame, you were so close."

He gets down to my level and grips my chin. "Tell me your name, little guinea pig." My tears continue falling down my face. I know I'm an ugly crier.

"Please, just let me get out and die free." He shakes his head at me.

"Little guinea pig, you will not die. You would have changed already. It's been two weeks. You're alive and well. With some side effects, of course. You're the hope of a new world."

He smiles at me, and I feel something in my stomach flip.

"Now tell me your name and I'll let you walk back. I might even consider not putting you under again if you agree to behave." I sit for a moment.

"Scarlet. My name is Scarlet," I answer softly, hoping he doesn't hear me. He extends his hand to me, but I slap it away and stand on my own.

"How did you find me so fast?" I ask. He takes my hand and lifts it up. Blood is still trailing down my arm.

"You left me breadcrumbs. But all the doors are locked like this. Can't risk someone getting in who doesn't belong, or someone important getting out." The last part he adds a smile to and gestures for me to lead the way. I do, but as I walk by, he grabs the badge from my hand and my head lowers in defeat.

After following the way I got down here, he escorts me back into my room and stays in the corner, planted in a chair. They hook me back up to everything. I sit with my hands in my lap, refusing to look at anyone. After a while, I lay on my side, refusing to go to sleep. What feels like hours pass by before he gets up. Thinking he's going to leave, I let out a breath of relief, but his footsteps come over to the bed. He tucks my hair behind my ear and everything in me sends alarms and warnings through my body. I take the opportunity and swing at him with my right hand. He grabs my wrists tightly. I wince at the pain as he grips me harshly. I bring up my other hand to try again. He catches that as well and holds them together above my head. I try to get my feet up to kick at him, but he has me pinned.

I continue squirming, trying to get away from him. He slams his mouth onto mine and closes mine tight. Tears run down my face. He forces my mouth open by biting down hard on my lip. When I cry out, his tongue goes into my mouth. I bite into his lip the same way he did mine. The taste of blood enters my mouth, making me want to gag. I refuse to let go.

He punches me in the side of my stomach, and I release. He checks his mouth and discovers the blood. I'm glad I made him bleed.

"Go to hell, dickhead." I spit what I have in my mouth on his face, calling him a sorry sack of shit. His face changes dark.

"God, I love a fighter. But you know what they say, an eye for an eye."

Not knowing what he is about to do, I thrash harder. I hear a flick and something sharp is at my side. I freeze, feeling the sharp cold tip of a knife. His voice is deathly calm.

"Keep your hands where they are or else I'll make it worse."

With that, he makes quick work of cutting the gown right down the middle of my chest. My nipples harden from the cold air. I beg him to stop, but it seems like it's only encouraging him.

Bringing the blade to my collarbone, he carves a line right below it. The knife slicing me sends a scream of pain stumbling out of my mouth. He shushes me like a child as he continues to carve something into me. The blade goes deep and slices through me like its nothing. I scream and beg him to stop, for someone to help me, but my cries go unanswered. Nobody is coming.

I apologize and swear to never run again, but he doesn't let up. He doesn't stop even for a second to consider my pleas.

The burning from the torture continues for what feels like hours, stretching across the right side of my chest.

After I'm covered in blood and my voice has gone mute, he declares he is finished. He bends down, licking the tender cuts, and I feel bile rise in my throat.

His hands harshly grab my waist and pull me lower onto the bed from where I was climbing it, trying to get away from him. I cry out for help. My voice is gone, and all comes out is a sorry excuse of my straining cry. in response to my cries, he slaps my face. The warning is understood as I let out a painful yelp. I try to plead and beg him to stop, promising not to run again if he just leaves. His hands move up and down my back, clawing into it. I bite at my lip to keep down the cries, fearing the absolute worst.

He doesn't like the reaction I'm showing. He grabs my hair at the scalp and my hands fly up to pry them out of the tangled mess.

Using the leverage, he slams my face against the rail of the bed. Once it makes contact, I cry out as everything goes hazy for a couple moments, making the feeling more intense. I don't even get a second to orient myself back to the event playing out before I hear a click. I try to hit him, but I'm stopped short by my wrist being attached to the restraints I forgot about. I pull and yank at my hands, trying to get free, and the more I do, the harder he slams against my ribs. My eyes shut tightly as I endure blow after blow. He stops for a second, demanding I look at him, but I keep my eyes squeezed shut. He grips my face painfully, forcing me to look him in the eyes.. I feel my eyes dim as I retreat into my mind. His eyes search my face and I stare at him as he does. When he's had enough of me, he undoes the restraints. Before flinging them away, I curl into a ball, scooting away from him and attempting to cover myself with the torn gown. The pain of the fresh injuries he's inflicted upon me is blinding.

"Come on, Scarlet. You didn't think you'd get away with running, did you? You needed to be punished. But next time, if you behave, you'll get an entirely different reward." He reaches for my face, and I hiss through gritted teeth when he meets the bruise that is forming. "So beautiful." He leans down and kisses my forehead, then walks out of the room like he didn't just torture me.

I don't sleep at all that night, and I don't plan to as long as I'm here. I don't know if this is the first time he's done this to me. If he's right, I've been here for two months, most of the time I've been unconscious.

I look at my reflection in the window and see what he carved. *Dominic*, in neat letters, now brands my skin.

Staying awake until the sun comes out is all I can do. I only have a sheet to cover myself with. When the two who first approached me after I woke up come in, they ask me what happened. I can't form words; I've shut down, staring off into space. They bathe me and dress me back into a new gown. I'm unable to move, so they have to carry me. I make it worse on them as I refuse to move.

The man who first carried me when I arrived shows so much compassion. I don't understand it. Why is he here? He takes time to whisper to me, telling me what he's doing while he's washing over me. He looks me in the face and asks if Dominic was the one who did this to me. My averted gaze tells him everything he needs to know, and he stops asking. The last thing he does is tend to the carving. It looks angry, almost infected. He makes it fast, I guess, so I don't have to look at it anymore.

# Chapter 13

## Oh, To Be Ignored

They start performing tests on me, taking samples and looking at various levels. Apparently, nothing has changed, except my cells now have a mutation. They have me go downstairs where some biter was being housed. After shoving me into the hallway, the infected ignores me, showing no want or interest. Taking advantage of I've been presented with, I go to the other side of the hall and sit down, refusing to leave. They try telling me and threatening me to return through the door, but I just stare at them as they do. The two people walk in to retrieve me and the infected goes crazy, screaming and throwing themselves at the door. Sounds of breaking bones ring out in the corridor as it tries to get to the meal it longs for.

Apparently they injected my blood into someone, and the person died within six hours. They couldn't handle the mutation process. They don't know why I'm different, and I honestly don't care.

After another week of Dominic's torment, I decide I've had enough and take the restraints from the bed and try to hang myself. The researcher, John, walks in and stops me. I am now on a 24/7 watch. I have a guard in my room, and I just stare at them. The hatred I feel makes them uneasy. I take my tiny victories as they come.

Dominic takes a shift every so often, and he uses that time to torment me. Looking at the wound that's healed, he talks about how I'm his now and he'll protect me. How we are special, the ticket to creating a new world. When he finds out about my attempt, he screams at me, slamming me into the wall. He makes me promise not to do it again before he throws me to the ground and kicks my stomach, breaking a couple ribs yet again

There's something wrong with him. He sticks around for a couple days and the beatings get worse.

The big one is when I tell him to kill me. He slams me against the wall by my throat. He then torments me again like he did that night, telling me I'm his fucking sicko.

I'm going to kill them.

I'm going to be the one who ends this.

# Chapter 14

## Markus

I watched as some strange figure ran with Scarlet on his shoulder. She screamed, and I tried to run after her, but I did not protect her. I failed to reach her.

We only saw the taillights of the vehicle and the license plate. Why did they grab her? We don't know where they took her, but we all agree we are getting her back.

Owen said the plate had a Philly decal on it. He noticed stickers on the black windshield, something about Penn state. So we can only hope that's where they're from.

We gather all our belongings. I attach Tank to my pants, and we take off as soon as day breaks. Jason's family agrees to join because Tommy's the one who let them find us.

We can't lose her after she's come to mean so much to us.

The joy she's brought to this dark world is something I can't live without. I will not live without.

We take off down the road in their RV, terror building with every mile. We arrive in the city in about six hours. The streets are quiet, and it makes no sense. We start off by looking for the car. We'll search every street if we have to.

## 2 weeks later

We've gotten to the east side of the city. Now biters are becoming denser, and we are close to the hospital. We are killing off at least ten a day. We've separated to cover more ground. Just as I was about to give up for the day, I saw a vehicle with the same stickers Owen described. The front is swarming with infected, but there the car sits. Right out front. The entire front seems to be barricaded by a metal rolling door. They pay no attention to it, just stumble around. I head back to the group to tell them about the discovery. Tank and Owen sit in the apartment we've taken over. I climb the fire escape to get up. As I walk in, Jack and Owen are whispering about something. I break the silence by announcing what I found, and relief crosses their faces. Jacob is asleep on the couch, so we'll fill him in later, but we start planning.

We won't get close enough to find a way in with all the infected present. We'll have to take them out, little by little, so hopefully we aren't noticed. We've changed base camp to a few buildings outside of the hospital. We see light on in there at night. Not a lot, but we know there are people there. Our first attack plan is simple: we go down and start chipping away at them silently, no loud weapons. Scarlet's bow sits unused in the corner. I've never shot one, but I think she wouldn't mind if I used it. The string is worn and fraying. I run my finger along where hers once sat. So much confidence in such a small woman.

I pull back the sting and smile at the size. It's a little small for me. I put it back down and we all head down the escape. Jack's staying with Tank for now. With our weapons in hand, we slowly leave the alley. I pick up a glass bottle and throw it against the wall. About three of them stumble into the alley. Me and Owen take our spots and hit them from behind. I plunge the end of my machete into the hard skull of the biter. It doesn't make a sound. As it falls, the loud drop of dead weight makes the last one stumble toward us. We wait for the moment it gets close enough. It bends down like it's smelling the fallen body. I raise my weapon and bring it down hard on its neck. Its head rolls and I cringe. We've got a long line of biters to get through. Scarlet just needs to hold out.

As we round the corner, we see a column of glass. We try the door and it doesn't budge. The door on the other side slams open. Running for cover, we all watch.

Scarlet is in a hospital gown, blood streaming down her arms. She looks thin and pale. The panic is clear as she slams her body against the door. The fire is gone, and something else is etched on her face. She throws her body at the door again and again before turning and hitting her back on the wall, sliding down. We can hear her wails.

My heart shatters at the sight. If we break the glass, we'd be swarmed with infected in two minutes. My arms flex, wanting to run over to her and tell her we're going to get her out.

A man walks down the stairs slowly. He looks to be calm and collected. Jack gets up, but I make him stay put. They are talking, but I can't hear the conversation. After a few minutes of him manhandling her, she gets up and walks back through the door. She looks defeated as her head hangs down. We all look at each other.

Jack has a look in his eyes that scares me. But now we know she's alive, so all we can do is work our way inside. We'll get to her, no matter how long it takes.

# Chapter 15

## Scarlet

I'm wheeled into some room. The place smells clean, almost sterile. Stainless steel and white make it an eyesore. They lock the door behind us and instruct me to get up on the exam table. As I stand, my legs wobbly from lack of nutrients, my eyes skim the area, finally settling on one side of the table where I see the restraints. I shake my head in protest. Dominic and some guy I haven't seen before pick me up under the arms and I kick, cursing them.

They slam me down on the table headfirst and Dominic grabs my throat. My hands fly up to his and hold at his wrist. The fear pumping through me has me in tears. I feel hands on my ankles and then smooth metal. I started kicking wildly with my left leg and I land one hit with the brief outburst. I receive an elbow to my knee, and I cry out, using the little air I've been granted. After they secure my ankles and thighs, they place one around my waist.

Dominic finally lets go of me and I try to get out. They pin my arms down and I pull away from them using the small amount of strength I have left, but it's always in vain. Trying everything to get loose, I beg them not to do whatever they are planning.

John walks up, and he has a sharp look on his face.

"I'm sorry, Ms. Scarlet, but we don't have the means to do this in a controlled environment. We will sedate you, but we need to know if the mutation has affected more than just your blood. I hope you can forgive us."

"No, you can't. This is fucked up, even for you guys."

I pull more wildly, and I see the guy I kicked has a mask in his hand. A mist of something is being released into the air. I move my head side to side, trying to make sure they can't sedate me.

Dominic grips my face and I hold my breath as the gas pours in. I refuse to breathe. John slams his fist into my leg, and I let out a cry, forgetting my mission of holding my breath. I take a deep breath. Everything becomes hazy. The last thing I see is John talking to Dominic.

# Chapter 16

## Scarlet

They didn't tell me what they did to me in that room, but frankly, I don't care. I don't want to know.

The tests have been getting more and more dangerous, not just for me. They have been trying to create a vaccine for me and it's making progress, but I hear them talking outside my door. Apparently, because they are getting so close, they don't want to risk me escaping, so Doc has ordered the entire faction to move. I can't even imagine what that means. Dominic's delusional state is becoming more and more concerning. I've learned if I play along, he doesn't get violent with me, so that's a plus.

The guard detail says they noticed a group of people close by and they were talking about pushing up the move to be on the safe side. I need to get out before that happens.

If I can make it down to the first floor again, I should be able to get out through the glass. I just need something to break the panes. The reason I didn't the first time was shock, I think. That and the whole "you're special" talk kind of set me off the deep end. I've been narrowing down the best time, and it seems at night. Certain guards don't care as much as others, so I can use that to my advantage. I just have to wait until one of them gets lazy enough to fall asleep, and then I'll make my move. The issue is that they don't carry weapons around me for some strange reason. Smart; if given the chance, I would happily go *Tomb Raider* on their asses. But once I can slip by them, it's a straight shot down the stairs, and instead of using the emergency exit, I'll go through the main lobby. I close my eyes, tired of pondering for now, and let sleep take me.

## Darkness

*"Scarlet, stop fighting it! This is childish. Why don't you see the reason?"*

*My father is screaming at me like always. After the last batch of subjects were terminated, I went catatonic, as the post doctor said. I've refused meals for four days now and apparently that is enough to get daddy dearest's attention.*

*I stare at him, my eyes hollow like always, and refuse to answer.*

*"This is your last chance. Now or you'll force my hand."*

*I look at the plate of food he brought with him and then return to him. Using my forearm, I swipe the tray off the small bedside table. The metal tray crashes to the ground with loud, ear-ringing noises. I match his stare, and I see sadness.*

*Too bad this monster can't actually feel anything. I'd almost believe him if I didn't know better.*

*I hear a click, and in an instant three of the security detail step into the room. I stand from my bed and look at all of them. My lips snarl in response. Bending down, I grab the tray I just swatted to the floor and hold it in front of me. I look innocent, but they've learned better by now.*

*"Scarlet. Don't make us do this," the head officer pleads with me. We've become close, but not close enough for him to fight*

*it. I cock my head at him. I haven't been able to form words since my "hunger strike," as my father calls it, started.*

*One of the additional guards clearly didn't listen to the briefing during his orientation and charges at me. I hit him in the stomach with the side of the tray, making him topple over. I slam it down on top of his head and almost made a dent in the stupid thing. He moans out from the massive headache he just received, and I toss the tray to the side. It clangs as it contacts the tile floor. I stand there staring at them, waiting to see what they do, and as always, they surprise me. They charge forward and get me on the ground. Two grab my arms and the third grabs my legs. I buck and try to wiggle out of their grasp. They take me out of my prison cell and head toward the med bay. I kick and swipe the entire way there and, of course, Father is right on their heels.*

*They place me on an exam table, holding me still. They buckle me down as they have many times before. I pull at the restraints, and they buckle my head in. The med bay doctor comes in and speaks to Father about something. I feel Luis stroking my hair and I look up at him. Sadness plagues his face. I give him a look of pleading, but he breaks eye contact with me just as quickly as I started it.*

*The doctor ends the conversation as he places a hand on Father's shoulder and walks over to me. My eyes go wild as I try to see what he's doing. He informs Luis to hold my head still. I try to scream out. I see a tube in his hand, and I try to make as much movement as possible, but the fluid holds me steady. I whimper and try to beg, but nothing comes out. He puts the tube right into my nose and instructs Luis to point my head back. I feel my neck strain slightly. He pushes the tube down my nose and I scream out. I feel the need to gag as it goes down and I fight harder, my eyes wide open, shooting over to my father as saliva and spit fly out of my mouth. "I'll fucking kill you for this.*

*All of you." My father turns away and walks out of the room, leaving me to whatever the hell this is.*

**Darkness**

A couple days have passed, and faking being asleep is the simple part. If they don't fall asleep by 1 am, then they won't, but one younger guy seems to think I'm harmless and scared, so he's the perfect person to underestimate me. Buying my time, I become more cooperative with them, hoping I can make them chill out a little more. Then the plan can start.

After testing and lots of blood draws, they finally send me back to my room with the younger guard. I fake a yawn and, as planned, he yawns. Laying down, I cover my face with my hair just enough so he can't see my eyes. I watch as his eyes become heavy, and he slowly spreads out and drifts drift away. Waiting the extra thirty minutes is the hardest part, but well worth it. As I look over at him, I drift the blanket off my body, my eyes never leaving him. I slide out of bed, making my way toward the door, shooting him one more hard look before poking my head out. Luckily, I don't see anyone. I bolt to the staircase across the hall, swinging open the door. I fly down the steps.

Just as I round one corner, I stop dead in my tracks, seeing a guard. I clearly surprised him; it shows on his face as he looks at me. It takes a minute to register what's going on for both of us, but just as I move, he snaps out of it. I turn around and fly upward. Continuing to the 6th floor, I bust into the hallway. As I do, three of the people that normally do testing on me look dead at me. One drops the deck of cards he was shuffling before I entered and I mutter "oh shit" before bolting past them. They all rush after me, chairs falling. They run over each other trying to get a footing.

Once I make it past them, I sling open the door and slam right into the wall before bouncing off. Heading into the opposite stairwell, I don't stop as a new rush of energy floods my body. I keep going until the 8th floor comes into view. I slow down just long enough to quietly slip in. I hear them rushing up and down the stairs in and out of floors.

Breathing, I take in my surroundings and look around. This looks like an office level. I slowly make my way forward.

I see a photo of me that looks like I was asleep when it was taken. I appear to look fuller and healthier than when I first arrived. There are notes and test results everywhere, scattered about on the next board, hung up with magnets. Blood type and different chemical levels, genetic make-ups, diets from childhood, and locations of developments, all trying to link something. I pick up a folder and see the front page: Progress notes.

name: Dominic king

Patient code: DK1765443

Age:27

weight: 210lbs

Blood type: O Neg

Code status: High priority.

Program findings age: 12-17

Pt. shows resistance to recent strands of virus present. Pt. DK1765443 along with Pt. SE1765493 show similar reactions.

Pt. AB1765447 and Pt. WB1765498 both presented expected results and had to be ended indefinitely from the program and code status. Pt. DK1765443 presents mental side effects and abilities that cause issues with detainment. When exposed to intimate partners, said partners became overly aggressive and had to be permanently ended, unlike counterpart Pt. SE1765493. Partners became more agreeable with Pt. SE1765493 and tried to help. Pt. SE1765493 breech containment.

Still clutching this one, I pick up the sheet next to it.

name: Scarlet Everglade

Patient code: SE1765493

Age:18

weight: 148.6lbs

Blood type: A Positive

Code status: High priority.

Program findings age: 06-18

Pt. shows resistance to recent strands of virus present. Pt. SE1765493 along with Pt. DK1765443. Counterpart has since breached containment and is no longer a practical subject for further rounds of test. Pt. stays fully operational, and progress continues to show improvement.

Show similar reactions. Pt. AB1765447 and Pt. WB1765498 both presented expected results and had to be ended indefinitely from the program and code status. Pt. SE1765493 is a danger to security as the effects of recent exposure partners became more agreeable with Pt. SE1765493 and tried to help. Pt. SE1765493 breech containment.

Everything becomes deathly silent as I drop the file, backing up. I twist around to run the opposite way but stop dead in my tracks, seeing Dominic breathing heavily in the doorway with an angry expression on his face.

"Do you remember the trials? I thought you looked familiar. You left me there. The only person I could connect with left. They tried to create another practical test subject, you know, but they were all failures, unlike the perfect little SE1765493. Although, I think you prefer Scarlet, right?"

He stalks toward me, forcing me to go back until I hit the edge of the table. My heart pounds in my ears as I push the memories back down to where they belong.

"I— I don't know what you're talking about."

He chuckles deeply as he runs his knuckles down my cheek. "You're such a liar. Scarlet, we all got the implants. You know that little area of raised skin that sits on your ribs, the one you tried to carve out but failed? SE1765493, something so meaningless to anyone else, but to us it was our lives. Did you know the old man Doctor Lucas was so excited when we figured out that the genetic code matched perfectly, and the test proved it all. He's excited to see you again, Scarlet."

Panic fills me at the mention of Doctor Lucas. That cruel man put me through so much, but he's supposed to be dead. I feel my hands sweating. "Please... Don't make me." My voice chokes out of me and the look in his eyes shows everything. To him, Doctor Lucas was like a father, but to me he was a cruel warden whose punishments still terrify me. I fall to my knees and grip onto his pants. "Please, Dom— You can't— Please don't make me."

I look up at him and beg him. The fear and terror that fill me is almost paralyzing.

"Scar, he misses you. He'll be so happy to know his little girl is coming home." He bends down to my level and cups my face. "I know it's been too long, but everything will work out just as it was supposed to. "

"No— He's dead. He died right before I escaped."

Panic consumes me and everything piles on at once. The wail that breaks out of my throat is something I've never heard. I feel the glass vibrate as I let it out. My throat burns and it feels like it's getting ripped apart. Some others run in but grab at their ears. Dominic, unfazed, stands up and grabs something from one of their pockets. He takes my forearm and does something. I feel my eyes roll and the pain goes away, the fear slips, the anxiety falters. My whole body relaxes, and I look hazily up at him. He picks me up and says something to the men before taking me back to my room. I lay there in a trance as he holds me and rubs circles into my back. After a few hours, I drift into sleep.

# Chapter 17

## You Never Truly Escape

*Blackness consumes me.*

*Hard leather straps tug at my wrists. I'm sitting on my knees and there is no light. I try to pick up my wrists but struggle to gain even an inch.*

*A door opens, and light floods inside to show a man standing there. The light hides all his features. He taunts me with my name. I know who he is, a monster who parades around like he is a God, weighing others' value in his sick, twisted trials.*

*No, no, no, no.*

*I start violently jerking against the restraints.*

*"Scarlet, darling."*

*I scream.*

*Out—*


*The cold metal stings my back as I lay there waiting for the white light to shine down on me. The monitor to my left beeps, reminding me I'm alive. The door latch clicks open, and my father enters, his white lab coat clean and pristine, his dark brown hair perfectly gelled back.*

*"Scarlet, why must you do this?"*

*I look at him, my eyes pleading.*

*"Please, Daddy, don't do this. I'm so sorry I went with Mom. Please."*

*He walks over and his knuckles stroke my face like they did when I was young. I lean into it.*

*"Scar, baby, I'm doing this to protect you. Your mother didn't understand."*

*My lip quivers. "Daddy, please— No." My voice cracks as tears crowd my eyes. He turns around and starts doing something. I don't know what, but from the recent experiences I've had, I know it's never good. Pain erupts in my arm and slowly spreads across my whole body. My back lifts from the burning, passionate feeling inside, and my eyes clamp closed.*

*Out-*

*The green trees are covered with pinks and purples as they bloom. Dom walks over to me and places his hand on my shoulder. I look up at him and he smiles at me gently. "Baby, why won't you just do as your father asks? I know the trials are painful, but they are what's expected."*

*I turn away and shake my head.*

*"You are a puppet, nothing more, nothing less."*

*Standing up, I turn and point a finger in his face. "My father uses you like a rag. We are not anything. I am not your baby, sweetheart, dark. Or love. You are a project my father forced me into from a young age, and I will not willingly give myself up to his sick new world plan."*

*His face goes dark. I hear the slap before I feel it. I hit the ground, catching myself with my hands. I touch where he just made contact. Looking at my hand, it goes dark.*

*Out-*

*"Dad, I'm sorry, please."*

*"Scarlet, disobedience is not tolerated. Running will not free you from this family's responsibilities."*

*He stands over me, towering over my place on the floor. The remote in his hand blinks a steady green, waiting for the command to activate. He presses the button and I feel electricity shoot throughout my body. I collapse to the floor and writhe in pain, begging for it to stop.*

*"Scarlet, I need you to just do as you're told. Why must you act like this?"*

*My body shakes and I feel exhausted. The pain cuts out as he lets go of the button. My breathing is rigid and I gasp for breath, pushing up on my hands. My legs are laying behind me. I glare at him and do something I've never done. "Fuck you, Lucas!" His face snaps into a cruel look, one I've never seen. He ignites the collar again and I slam to the floor. Screams break out of me, my eyes roll back, and my body becomes tense. He stops for a second, only to keep going. After three more pulses, I feel a burning in my chest. It follows up into my throat on the third shock, when he finally allows release. I slam my hands on the ground and let out a blood-curdling scream. "I've had enough!" I scream until I feel the burn pass out of my throat. Tears fall from my eyes. I watch as my father drops to the ground, covering his ears. The room looks like it's shaking, but I can't stop. I see blood slowly trail out of where his hands are. I feel my lungs constrict and it all goes silent.*

*I crawl over to him slowly. I approach his body, which stays curled into a ball. Turning him over, I look in disbelief. "Daddy?" Just as I do, the door bursts open, and I'm tackled to the ground by two men. They force my arm out and sedate me like they often do. I killed my father. Why am I not sorry? Why am I sad?*

# Chapter 18

## Dominic

Looking over the results, my heart swells. It's her. After all these years, it's her. We knew she was alive, but I didn't think we'd ever find her again.

We were trying to continue the trial for a vaccine, and the one we stumbled upon was here. When we were talking to that boy, I didn't know. Almost everyone here is from the facility. When it finally clicked into place, a lot of the staff seemed overjoyed at the discovery. We sent word to Doctor Lucas, and he instructed us to pack up and come back to the bunker. She is the key.

All we have to do is get her back and everything will be fixed. The point of the trials was to make a species that could naturally be immune to all current viruses and bacteria. But despite our many efforts, one transport container of a virus was damaged, causing the infection to spread wide at a speed we couldn't control. The havoc was awful. Finding a new match for her was crucial, but now we have her. After years of looking and her trail going cold, we actually found her. We're packing up all the material to head back. As I gather up the documents to return, the fire alarm goes off.

The policy set in place was so if there was a potential breach, the lights would signal, but the noise was cut. She's attempting to escape again. I bolt from my office and hit the stairwell, running down to the first floor. I hear yelling above me. I look up and three floors above are two of my men.

I tell them to stop and rush up. They inform me she ran past them but went up. I instruct them to cover the roof down and I will make my way up to them. Entering the 6th floor, the dark is illuminated by the flashing lights and the floodlights that help manage power. I check every room: nothing is out of place and dust is thick in the air. But when I get to the 8th floor where my office sits, I slowly open the door and I see her in the hospital gown staring down at one of the many files I have in the room.

I stop in the doorway, watching her for a second. She holds my file in her left and picks up her own in her right. After a quick moment of reading the last entry, she drops them both and shakes her head. She spins around and my breathing shows how hard I was pushing myself to track her down. I speak, wanting to see if she'll deny what we both know.

"Do you remember the trials? I thought you looked familiar, and you left me there. The only person I could connect with left. They tried to create another test subject, you know, but they were all failures, unlike the perfect little SE1765493. Although, I think you prefer Scarlet, right?" I walk forward, matching her every step until she's stopped by the table.

"I– I don't know what you're talking about."

I chuckle to myself.

She didn't know what she did when she left me. When she left the facility, we scrambled to find her or someone like her, but we couldn't. "You're such a liar, Scarlet. We all got them. You know, that little implant that sits on your ribs, the one you tried to carve out but failed. SE1765493, something so meaningless

126

to anyone else, but to us it was our lives. Did you know the old man Doctor Lucas was so excited when we figured out that the genetic code matched perfectly, and the test proved it all? He's excited to see you again, Scarlet."

I see the fear in her eyes. Toward the end, she became more hostile toward me. The last time they did a trial together, she almost killed him with that scream of hers. We called her Banshee after that; she busted his ear drums.

"Please... Don't make me."

Her voice is unrecognizable as she falls to her knees, gripping my pants. The fear shows. I know that fear. Back at the beginning, when she just took it, I fought. The only reason I stopped was because I realized I had nowhere to go.

"Please, Dom— You can't— Please don't make me."

The way she looks breaks my heart, but I can't deny him if we want this to be over.

"Scar, he misses you. He'll be so happy to know his little girl is coming home." I bend down to her and try to comfort her, hoping she can understand he has changed with age. He was urgent about getting her home because he sees the chaos of being his only child. He doesn't want her out here. "I know it's been too long, but everything will work out just as it was supposed to." I smile at her sweetly.

"No— He's dead. He died right before I escaped." After her first episode with that banshee scream of hers, the doc was under sedation while he healed. She busted out his eardrums and nearly killed him.

The wail that breaks out of her throat is something I haven't heard in a long time. My eardrums are more equipped for her banshee call than others'.

My ability adds a shield, making me able to withstand more. I try to calm her down, but she curls into herself, grabbing her hair and rocking back and forth on her knees. Some more staff run in but grab at their ears, falling to the ground. Leaving her for a second, I walk over and dig through one of their pants, looking for the sedation. Finding it quickly, I go back to Scarlet, take her arm, and inject the liquid.

As her eyes roll back, her entire body relaxes. I catch her before she falls over and she glances up at me like she used to. The look in her eyes is tired and defeated, but we need to prepare for departure. I stand up with her in my arms and tell the men to be ready in the morning when we are leaving. Slowly, I walk to her room down the steps. The alarm has finally been turned off. Once we get there, I can't let her go. She lies on my chest as she falls asleep.

In a trance-like state, she tunes everything out. John walks in and informs me everyone will be ready to go as soon as the day breaks. The herd outside had been dwindling, so they loaded everything out through the loading bay. We both decide it would be best to transport her medicated because of the risk of her leaving again. He goes and grabs the doc, who administers a sedative through her IV, and we hook up the feeding tube yet again. Restraining her, we set up one ambulance for the trip. We leave her for the night, prepped and ready to go. We discuss the route; it will take four days with the entire convoy of supplies we have to take back.

After planning throughout the night, we load Scarlet. After we transfer her to the stretcher and attach the harness, we double-check that the IVs are fully charged along with the backups, ensuring we can swap out during the trip. Me and Doc will be with her, and John will drive. To finish tying up loose ends, we execute the testing group of the remaining staff we'd captured when we arrived. Their dead eyes are something I won't miss when we go back underground.

After a last check, we all load up and get ready to leave. Scarlet is making noises as we roll her out. Her face tightens and relaxes, and I assume she is dreaming. Once the group fully clears the first floor, we take the elevator down. The numbers have dwindled to a low number. I stop and look around the glass-covered room that at one point was swarming with the infected. They are all gone. It makes no sense.

I tell Doc and John to wait as I pull my pistol. Looking around, I step toward the front entrance and an arrow lands right in front of me, stuck in the door.

I dive behind a desk and peek out. There are three men, all with muscular builds. One has a large ax, another has a melee weapon I can't place strapped to his back and has loaded another arrow, and the last one is welding a machete. The dead have thinned out and are no longer a threat to the three. I look at John and tell him to load Scarlet onto the bus. I watch as they approach the door. Instead of trying to open it, they shatter the glass and step through.

"Can I help you, gentlemen?" I say from my hiding place.

The one with the bow speaks. "We want our friend back."

So, this is the group she was traveling with. How they found us, I don't care, but I'll be damned if I'm giving her up.

"I don't know who you're talking about. Can I get a description?"

Another one speaks up. "Yeah, our Firefly, the one we saw trying to get out covered in blood. Ring a bell?" How long have those fuckers been here planning this?

"What if I told you she was dead?"

It goes quiet for a minute. Nobody moves, but I hear the hammer of a gun get pulled and a spray of ammo fills the desk. I roll away and they hit me, but it doesn't go far. I can repair it later. I stand up and return fire. They scatter like the rats they are, and I hear yelling from my men. I yell into the air to get the trucks running and take off toward the loading bay. I hear their footsteps behind me as I am bound to my destination. I turn a corner fast and one of them slams into it.

John and Doc already have her loaded. I can see her strapped in. Her gorgeous features push me harder. Doc stands with the door open, yelling at me to hurry.

I see Scarlet in all her glory, strapped up and hooked to everything needed in order to transport her safely. I hear bullets yet again and John yells before falling back. He slides out of the truck and starts screaming. I jump over him and into the truck, closing one door as I go. When I reach for the second, Doc's hand is in the way. I look down at him, then at the people only feet away. I shoot him in the arm, leaving him for the infected, and slam the door closed. The truck speeds forward and I'm slammed against the door.

Everything moves and shifts. I see them in the window. One attacker raises his gun and sprays bullets at the vehicle. A large bang shatters the silence, and the truck becomes lopsided. It rides a second longer before flipping. I watch as Scarlet's stretcher slings across the cab.

# Chapter 19

## Markus

We stand at the glass entrance, ready to move. We've seen them packing trucks in a rush and we must act now. I pull back the string of the bow as I see three figures pushing something through the waiting area. One of them stops. He's large and stands on edge. He looks around and makes his way toward the entrance slowly. As he turns, I release the arrow and it hits its target, going right through the door. It stops short, right at his eyes. I watch as he dives behind an overturned desk. Me, Owen, and Jack walk forward. As we approach the door, Owen raises his ax and shatters it before stepping through. As we follow, our chests rise and fall in sync, feeling the adrenaline pumping. The man behind the desks speaks.

"Can I help you, gentlemen?"

Gentlemen? What does he think, this is a fucking tea party? I speak out, trying to keep my voice from shaking.

"We want our friend back. "

"I don't know who you're talking about. Can I get a description?"

Owen speaks up this time. Harsh and to the point. "Yeah, our Firefly, the one we saw trying to get out covered in blood. Ring a bell?"

He takes a couple of moments before filling the silence, telling us she's dead. Jack cocks back the gun he now has a death grip on and sprays right into the desk. We wait a second before taking a step, but to our surprise the guy pops up and returns fire. We scatter for cover and he runs down the corridor. We don't hesitate as we follow him.

Owen slams into the wall as he turns a corner, and we see an open loading bay of an ambulance as we push ourselves. I see Scarlet. There are tubes connected throughout her. He's got her hooked up to machines and out cold. I feel myself pushing harder, trying to get to him. Jack raises the gun and lets it rip. I expect him to hit the douche we're chasing, but he aims for the man in the doors, hitting his target. The guy falls. He slides out of the ambulance and the screaming is heart-shattering. The target we are trying to catch leaps into the ambulance and slams the door. As he tries to close the second one, he's stopped short by a man's hand gripping tightly to the door frame. Without a second thought, he aims and shoots him in the arm, causing the poor bastard to let go. He slams the door closed and the ambulance takes off. Jack opens fire and hits the back left tire.

The truck becomes unbalanced, and with the high speeds it flips. We watch in horror as it rolls not once but twice, landing on its side. We all look at each other, and it takes a moment to set in: We stopped it. Holy shit, we stopped it!

We hug one another, sending out whoops and cheers. Our celebration is cut short when Owen speaks up.

"Wait, Scarlet!"

We all take off toward the truck, Jack being the first one at the door. He slams it open, and we are met with an awful sight. Blood and fluids cover the area. I crouch down and look at the guy we chased, slouched over and pinned against the wall by a stretcher. Equipment and supplies are scattered around. We see an arm in the doorway toward the front. I set my focus on the stretcher: Scarlet is still harnessed in and knocked out. I make quick work of unclipping them and push the stretcher away from her. Me and Jack grab her ankles and slide her out. There's blood coming from her nose and arm where I guess they had her hooked up. She's skinny and frail-looking. Her cheeks seem hollow, and her curves are less prominent.

The gown she is in hangs loosely around her shoulders. Her blonde hair is soaked in blood. We try to wake her up, shaking her for some kind of response. She does nothing, but I feel a pulse and let out a relieved sigh

"Guys, we need to go now!" Owen says. There is a group of the infected rounding the corner, targeting the man whimpering and crying. Jack throws Scar over his shoulder, and we take off back through the building, quickly navigating the halls. Some stragglers have found their way in and are wandering aimlessly about. We bolt past them only to hear their screams as we do.

We make it to the front entrance, never slowing down as we bound down the street. Rounding the corner, we cut into the alley that has the apartment we've been staying in.

The ladder is pulled down and Owen is the first to go up. Jack follows with Scarlet draped over his shoulder. He uses one hand to pull himself up, causing it to take a little longer. I'm right on his ass, checking behind me every few seconds to make sure I'm not about to get completely swarmed. When he's about halfway up, I hear the screams approaching. Once we get up, Owen bangs on the closed glass. Jacob comes rushing out of the other room and throws open the window. Jack hands her through before joining them inside. Tank instantly recognizes her and starts jumping up trying to get to her, his tail moving a million miles a minute. We explain what happened back there: the baffling guy, the ambulance, how we almost lost her for good. Jacob looks mortified. Clutching her limp form to his body tightly, he refuses to let us take her back into the room so she can get some sleep. The sadness on his face as he holds her breaks my heart. He's always been the most sensitive out of all of us. After a while, we convince him to lay her down on the bed. We look over her injuries. Bruises and cuts cover her body, but when we see a name carved into her skin, we stand back. Bile rises in my throat.

"Dominic" is carved into her. The scar looks angry and deep. Guilt spreads through me. If we only worked faster, we could have stopped this. We talk for a while about what to do. Tank has refused to leave the bed where she lays, cuddling into her like he did when he was a puppy. The safest choice is to get away as soon as possible. The baffling guy, for all we know, only got knocked out, and the sooner we get away, the safer she will be. We talk about waiting until the sun rises and, whether she's awake or not, getting the hell out of here and moving north. Far away from this godawful city.

We load all our stuff into the SUV we found and load Scarlet into the back seat. Tank sticks to her like glue. Covering her up with a blanket, we load in ourselves. I place myself in the back with her. Her head rests in my lap. I stroke her hair as I stare down at her. Jacob volunteers to drive and we talk about heading to Michigan, trying to pass the time. The cold will help slow them down if they try to come after her.

After a couple hours on the road, Scarlet stirs awake. We watch as her eyes open slowly, but the look in her eyes is one of terror and panic. She slams her hands against me, throwing all her weight into me. I hit the seat with my back. Her hands go around my throat, and she tightens her grip. Jacob stops in the road and throws the car into park. I try to dig my fingers in between her grip, but her eyes don't show my Firefly. They look like they are dead, like autopilot has taken over. Jack grabs her from behind. She rips off me and leaves scratches on my neck. She kicks and screams, clawing back at Jack's face. He secures her arms and shushes her. He falls back onto the ground and wraps his legs around hers. I hear him shushing her and he rocks back and forth. He whispers that she's okay now, that we got her back.

She takes a moment to notice where she is, and her face shoots to look at me. Tears well in her eyes, and I cradle her face in my hand. "I told you, Firefly, you're safe." She latches onto me, bawling and wailing. I take her from Jack, but not before he tries to refuse. I hold her tightly into me as she lets it all out; her hands grip my shirt for dear life. Tank slowly approaches and nudges his nose at her. She turns around from me and hugs his neck, talking about how he's such a good boy and how she missed him. Jack sits up from the seat and talks about how he was a good boy, but his treatment wasn't nearly as nice. A small smile cracks on her face and she just sits on the floor petting Tank. She doesn't say a lot to us, just a small thank you before she shuts down completely.

# Chapter 20

## Some Are Better Kept In the Dark

Since they all came and rescued me, I have said little. They've been pushing me to eat more, but I can barely stomach the few bites I've gotten down. Tank is now attached to my hip, and Markus is always touching me. They had some of my clothes from my pack and I changed into them.

It feels weird to be outside, but we haven't stopped moving. I don't know exactly where we are. We headed west and stopped at a house that looked untouched to scrounge around for food. The biters have changed in ways that none of us can explain. We've discovered what we call "watchers." They go ahead of the herd and just stare at you. If you get too close, they let out this feral scream. They don't attack, but they run. The scariest thing is how fast they are.

The weather has turned cold, and I've been wanting to find a sweater for Tank, but the boys make fun of me for it. We pull up to a townhouse, park the car, and exit one by one. I see the family we were with when I got kidnapped and they come out to greet me. Rose throws herself into my arms and starts pouring out everything that has happened. We have a quick hello before loading up into their RV. We don't stay there any longer than it takes to pack up their supplies

Tommy stays to himself, not saying a single word. Jason is driving, and I'm sandwiched between Markus and Jack. My eyes grow heavy as we go down the road. The storm isn't really getting any better, but we really don't have a choice. We can see the infected slowly moving in a field. Rose clamps to her sister Beth, trying not to look. Tank lays in between my feet, suckling on a teddy bear Rose gave him. We discuss where we need to go, and it gets brought up how hard the storm is going to hit soon. We stay on the road as long as possible using abandoned roads as markers. After a few hours, we see buildings that have been destroyed. Apparently some local governments started bombing high-infected areas, trying to kill off as many as possible.

We see a little townhouse that's not nearly as bad as the others. The roof has collapsed in, but the walls still stand tall. We pull over and debate whether we stay in the RV or go inside. Jason points out that we need to see if there is anything valuable, and most of us agree. I step out of the RV and the strong wind hits me. Tommy follows along with Jacob and Markus. We do our usual sweep. The cold of the house makes my fingertips hurt and burn all at the same time.

We find some nonperishable food and sodas. Jacob and Markus fight over who should get one and I chuckle at the intensity of the debate. After a while, they decide to wait it out and ask Jason who should get one. They walk our findings back to the RV and I look around for anything material-wise that's useful. I'm shuffling through the closet and Tommy is somewhere in the house. As I pull out some linen to see if anything is behind them, I'm pulled from my task by a loud crash coming from inside. Me and Tommy look at each other. I grab a kitchen knife and slowly go to where the noise was.

There's a basement door we didn't check when we swept the first time. Before opening the door, I look at Tommy. He grips his bat for dear life. I open the door and the wind picks it up, slamming it against the wall. I hear a short screech that almost sounds panicked. Loud, angry steps tear through the basement. The infected throws itself into the walls as it scampers up the stairs. Its head slams into the concrete wall. I take a few steps back, preparing for a fight.

The biter grips onto the door frame, its head poking out, turning from left to right. It goes silent. I hold my breath, hoping it can't hear me. Its hands stretch across the door, its palms gliding across the wooden surface, old blood leaves marks in its wake. I look at Tommy and motion for him to go. He doesn't move. I stare at the bite. This one is different; it doesn't see us right away. The eyes are milky, blood seems to have poured from around them. It's not moving like some others would. I take a slow step back. The ragged breath of the infected makes my goosebumps rise. I make my way to Tommy and touch his shoulder. He's shaking. I use my hands to turn him toward the back door. As I do, it's like fight-or-flight kicks in. He takes off through the house. His loud footsteps make the biter snap its head toward Tommy. He slams open the back door, sending the thing into a frenzy. Its movements are uncoordinated and volatile, tripping over everything just to go after Tommy.

I trail behind them, watching the two run across an open field of snow. The biter leaves a trail of crimson and I push myself to catch up. I see trees in the opening and Tommy is heading straight for them. I pull off my bow and line my shot. Taking in a deep breath and stopping for a moment, I release the arrow and it slams into the biter's back. It screams in what I guess is pain and whips around from side to side, trying to figure out where I am. It tries to get to the arrow that's now imbedded in its back, jerking back and forth, its arms flailing behind it. I pull back the string again and raise my aim slightly, adjusting for the drop. I line it up and hit the biter in the head. It twirls from the force of the arrow. I run to the biter and investigate. Blood clots cover its nose and seem to bulge out of its eyes. I pull out my arrows and wipe them off on the biter's clothes.

This thing used only sound. It didn't have the slightest exact location, but it knew general direction. I guess in a panic someone would scream and it would find its target, almost like a deadly game of Marco Polo. I load up another arrow and track Tommy's steps quickly. I stomp through the snow. The cold is bitter and hurts my ears. I see his tracks slow for a minute and then speed up again after a while. This idiot can run. I hear something break and I fly around, pulling the string back, ready to launch an attack. When I see nothing, I slowly back away. I move away from the source of the noise and look back to the tracks, now slowly filling with snow from the storm. I pick up my pace so I don't lose it.

A hut comes into view as I look around, trying to keep my eyes on the tracks but also not wanting to get ambushed. I follow them to an opening right before the lodge and there is a large area of packed snow where I guess a fight broke out. I follow larger footprints that seem to meet up with two more. All three are large and heavy, but the ones on the side make a deeper indent, showing me they probably picked up Tommy and carried him. I make my way, crouching, trying to avoid being seen, toward the area where they lead. There are three black vehicles outside. I notice the snow doesn't settle on them, but melts away, telling me they're still hot from running. A crunch comes from the other side, and I quickly duck down and listen to them talking.

"So that's the kid? He doesn't look like much to me. His group better be worth all this hassle."

Another voice speaks up. "I think this entire trip was a waste of resources. But we need to get the boy talking." I listen as they walk away, into the house, and the door slams shut. I slowly stand and hear a movement to my left. I look back. There's someone in the truck's bed. They throw themselves over and land on the ground with a soft crunch. Pulling back my bow, I ready a shot. The man grabs onto my weapon and yanks it out of my grip. I go with it and roll, looking up. My hair is in my face, so it's hard to see him, but what I can see is that this man is built like a beast.

He stalks toward me, and I grab my knife from its holster. Having the blade point out toward my elbow, I run at him and slash, getting his arm. He tries to grab at me but misses. I slide on the snow and charge again. He goes to hit me, and at the last moment I lose my footing and slam on the ground. I slash up his leg and he squats to grip the injury. Blood pours out, and I feel baffling but amazing. I yell, "Get up and fight me."

He stands and I can feel the anger rolling off him in waves. He pulls out his own knife and tries to stab me. His movements are blocky and rigid. I dive under his legs, using the packed snow to my advantage. Turning on my back, I kick at the back of his knee and he goes down. I quickly fumble to my feet and jump on him. He stands, trying to pull me off; as he does, one of his hands gets ahold of my hair, and he tries to use it to sling me off. I yell out right before I dig my blade into his shoulder, slashing in and out. I finally the right spot, where his shoulder meets his neck, and I turn the blade right in that pressure point. He screams and grabs ahold of my jacket, flinging me off him. I tumble and roll, my knife sliding away from me. I quickly scramble to get to it, but he comes running at me and pulls back his leg as if to kick me.

His boot slams into my stomach, and I groan at the impact. My body turns away; he takes the opportunity and grips onto my ankle, pulling me somewhere. I claw at the ground, only getting handfuls of snow and gravel. Using everything in me, I twist my body around, making him lose his grip. My ankle screams in pain at the motion. Gritting my teeth through the pain, I crawl back to where my knife is and quickly grab it. I slice my hand in the process, but I pay no attention as I crawl up to stand. I charge at him, jumping onto his back, yet again he spins me around. I take a second, but I line up the blade and slice across his neck, then pull it back and stab at his back again.

He falls to the ground, sending me sliding. I jump back, coming to rest in a crouched position, ready for more, but what I see is gruesome. Blood pours out of his wound, showing me I hit the right spot. I hear a gurgling, and he clutches at his neck, trying to say something. The blood is hot compared to the snow, and it steams as it spills onto the white blanket. I know my jacket is covered, probably everything else as well.

Clutching the blade, I wipe it off on his clothes, and as I do, he grips onto my wrist tightly and I watch as his eyes fade. Genuine fear shows in his eyes, and I feel a rush like I've never felt before. He lets go. Throwing myself back, quick deep breaths plague my body as I try to ground myself. I check his body, looking for something useful. I lift his shirt and find a gun tucked away. Why didn't he just shoot me? Would have made his life easier. I laugh at my inside comment, and with the pistol in hand and the knife at the ready, I stalk up the stairs and kick open the door. It slams against the wall and I see two men. I shoot one in the shoulder and he falls to the ground with a grunt. I turn quickly toward the other man and fire off a shot. I miss his shoulder by inches and he dives behind a couch. I stalk forward, continuously shooting. Fabric and cotton flies into the air and I soon hear the *click click* of an empty clip Throwing it to the side, I leap over the couch and land with a loud thud, knife ready...but nothing and no one is there. I look around for the person I just shot at. The man I shot grunts as he pulls himself up. I walk over to him and slam my foot against his back. He falls forward and I flip him around, putting the blade against his throat. I speak in a voice that is cold and full of hate. "Where is the kid?" The man struggles against me.

"I'm going to ask again. If you don't answer me, I'm going to slice your throat and watch you bleed. Where is the kid you all just grabbed?" I demand, my face inches away from his.

"We did nothing wrong. We just wanted to ask him if he knew anything about the survivors out here or if he's seen any valuable resources. That's it. We were going to let him go!" I lean closer to his face. I can almost feel the fear coming off him.

I whisper into his ear, "Fucking liar." Just then, an arm goes around my neck and I'm pulled off the man. I kick and scratch. Bringing the knife back, a hand grips my wrist and squeezes. The pain goes deeper and deeper and I think he's about the break my wrist when my hand gives out and the weapon goes clattering to the floor. I bring my head back and slam it into the stranger's nose. He lets go of me, stumbling back. I launch myself at him, punching him straight in the face, my hand throbbing from contact. I shake it, not realizing how painful it is to actually hit someone. The man quickly recovers from my hit and tackles me to the floor. I quickly scratch at anything I can.

His hands go around my throat and I get even more pissed off. I go weak as black dots cloud my vision, but he lets go of my neck and grabs my wrist, sitting on top of my hips. I look up at the stranger: strong jaw, blues eyes, brown hair, slight stubble, and there's a scar across his face going over his left eyebrow to his right check down the bridge of this nose. He's built like a tank and tall. I tell him to get the fuck off me and he just looks at me with an unreadable expression.

A loud slam comes through the door and a kid around Tommy's age is yelling. "Dude, Ricardo's dead. Someone slaughtered him!" He looks at the mess I've caused and the situation we're currently in, and his face goes into an expression that is tough to decipher. "She did this?" He seems stunned.

The man I was about to kill speaks up. "She's a fucking psycho!"

I roll my eyes. "I told you I wouldn't hurt you if you told the truth." I look up at the big burly man holding me down. "So, while I have you here, where is Tommy?"

He looks at me, puzzled. "Who?"

"Tommy, the kid you all snatched up maybe 30 minutes ago!"

"I'm over here, Scarlet." I crane my neck back to see an upside-down Tommy standing at the steps that lead to the second floor. Anger runs through my veins, and I somehow get unlatched from the man and crawl toward him.

"I just got fucking attacked, shot a man, and tried to kill another, and you're fine and dandy?" I crawl toward him, pulling the man with me. He chuckles at me and pins my arms down again.

"You're a feisty one."

I growl in annoyance. "Why the hell did I risk my life running after your childish, ungrateful ass? I should have let the blind

143

biter—" I turn my head to the man. "Can you get off me so I can go kick his ass?"

The man looks at me like I grew three heads. "No. Josh, grab me the rope." At that, my eyes go wide. I squirm against the man, trying to pry my way out. He forces my arms behind my back and ties off my hands.

Securing my ankles, he tightens them as well. "Uh, Tommy, right, get in the truck. We're going to get your family."

I throw curse after curse at them, and eventually he gets annoyed and gags me. All I can make out is a very loud murmur to him. They throw me in the truck and Tommy directs them exactly where to go. The RV comes into view after a short 15-minute drive. They unload and there are eight of them, not including Tommy. They check the RV and it's empty. Walking inside, they throw me on the ground. Everyone stands up, ready to fight. The girls all go behind my men.


One thug who pulled me in here speaks up. Everyone looks at him bewildered. "Hello, my name is Dean, and you have formally been recruited into the BIO division. Only the strong can join our ranks. Please hand over your weapons or we will have to take extreme measures." He speaks like this is something they do every day, and when nobody moves an inch, he crouches down and removes the gag from my lips.

"This is your last chance. Do as I say or, sadly, I'll have to take drastic measures."

I tell him to go get head from a biter and he shrugs his shoulders.

"Fair enough. The hard way it is. "

Before I can get off another insult, he slams a knife into my thigh, and I let out a string of curse words. The blade sits there for a second before he rips it back out and a scream leaves my lips in response.

Slowly, everyone lowers their weapons and does as they are told, kicking them across the floor. A man built like Markus, but much taller, steps from behind us. He throws a disgusted look my way and approaches the group.

Going down the line, he tells people to step forward.

Beth-step forward.

Rose-stay.

Jason-forward.

Laila-forward.

Markus-stay.

Jack-stay.

Jacob-forward.

Owen-stay.

Clarissa-forward.

Chris-stay .

He gives a nod and they zip-tie everyone. The people who were told to step forward all at once get pushed and shoved outside. We stare at the group. Frank gives me a weak smile before he leaves the house. Not a second goes by before multiple shots ring in the air. Echoes of screams come out from the silence that follows. Tank is posted beside Rose with a growl. One guy grabs his fur and muzzles him with tape. He whimpers at this and my heart breaks. I look at Tommy, who is standing still, shocked at what just happened.

Anger pulls out of me, along with tears. "You fucking caused this! You are fucking dead, do you hear me? Fucking dead!" I scream at Tommy.

The man from before who stabbed me in the leg walks over and cuts the ropes holding me. I clamber against the ground. I pull myself outside and I see the massacre before me. All the bodies lay in the snow. Pulling myself over to Jacob, I pull him onto my lap and wail out in anger. This can't be real. I just got them back. They just got me back. I can't make sense of what just happened. I slap his face twice, looking for any sign of life. Markus, Owen, and Jack crowd around me. They fall to their knees, and we mourn our friend. He's heavy and I struggle to pull him to my chest, so I lower myself to him. Disbelief rings through my soul, the cold snow bites at my knees, and I can't pull myself from him.

Then I see Rose in the doorway. Her face goes pale and she runs to her fallen family. I let go of Jacob and throw myself toward her. I get her jacket and pull her into me. She's fighting me, telling me we need to check on them. I push her head into my chest and try to soothe her. I tell her to calm down. We rock back and forth as she gives in and clings to my jacket, peering at her grandparents and siblings and cries harder. Chris, her older brother, is in a state of shock looking over everyone. He can't break his eyes away. As he stands there, one man from their group comes out behind him, speaking like nothing happened. He instructs everyone to "load up." We all just look at him, nothing registering.

When nobody moves, he mumbles something under his breath, pushes past Chris in his empty-like state, and stomps over to me. He grabs Rose's jacket and rips her out of my arms. I scream out at him. Still unable to stand, I grab something hard from the ground and throw it at the guy holding her. Using all my strength, I throw myself up off the ground. Pain radiates from my injured thigh and my step falters as I try to advance toward him. Within seconds, I'm thrown off course by the man who decided who lived and who died and we slide on the ground.

He climbs on top of me, his fist slams into my face, and I put my arms up to protect myself. I feel the crunch as my forearm breaks. I scream out. As I do, his fist comes down and hits me, stunning me. My world spins. They drag Markus toward their convoy and I feel my body sliding against the cold snow-covered earth. The bodies are left to lay. I try to stop them, but my arm feels hot from the break, and all I can do is beg as I watch the others stand and follow. My blood is roaring and pulsing in my ears. They throw us in the back of a large moving truck. Closing the hatch, we sit there with at least two of the men as they zip-tie our wrists together.

The wound on my leg has already started mending itself, but they don't know that. I feel the temperature in my leg rising. Tommy is back here with us; he keeps his head down. "I hope you are so proud of yourself," I say, venom thick in my voice. He ignores me but turns away.

Jack tries to step in. "Scar, he couldn't have known—"

I interrupt him. "Known what? That he was putting the entire group at risk? That he would get his family and Jacob killed." My voice rises. "Ignorance is no longer bliss in this world, Jack. Ignorance gets you and the people you love killed, mutilated, or turned into a meal." I feel my rage building. "Last time I was ignorant enough to do anything alone, I was separated from my original group. I got kidnapped and beaten to a pulp. In this world, those risks he took on that radio killed them. And I want to hear him admit it."

Jack tries to defend Tommy, but Markus joins my side. "Jacob is dead, Jack, and now Rose only has him, Chris, and us. The only reason these pricks came here was to find Tommy's location."

A guy in the back who kept quiet snickers. My head snaps at him.

"Oh, it's your fucking fault too, buddy. Don't think I forgot. You better ask your friend Ricardo what I'm capable of, because I'm going to gut you worse than any biter, but I'll leave you alive so you can feel every ounce."

The truck falls silent and the man I just threatened storms to where I am. He grabs me by the front of my shirt and lifts me up. "Is that a threat, whore?"

My eyes darken at the insult. I bring my head back and slam it into his. He drops me and stumbles back.

Unable to do anything, I scoot back and look down, realizing I need to calm down. The second man who's in here with us tells him to chill out, saying how Dean would be pissed if he finds out about that outburst. The rest of the ride is deathly quiet, mostly filled with me glaring daggers at Tommy. The two in charge of us chitchat about getting home. I make my way over to Markus and lay my head on his shoulder, trying my best to comfort him.

When we arrive, we hear lots of noise outside and two bangs come from the door. The men respond with four and the hatch opens. We are blinded by the bright light of the sun. Outside, I see a group of three men. The one who first introduced himself as Dean stands there proudly, and two more stand behind him. We are instructed to stand up, and we follow orders. With my leg being injured, I can't, so I sit there. The guy who stopped the douchebag from attacking me comes over and picks me up. I try to keep as much distance as I can from this guy. He jumps down with me, and I look around. A sign reads *Welcome to Little Falls.* The square is a line of shops that cover both sides, and where we just entered looks like they built a giant metal gate. Making our way down the road, there are people everywhere. Heading toward city hall, we're ushered into an office space and there sits a man looking something over. I'm placed in a chair and everyone else stands. The man puts down his paper and looks at us. He's older, with graying hair slicked back to perfection. He's thin and looks like age hasn't done nearly as much damage as it should have to him. Stubble grows on his face, and he has wrinkles beside his eyes. "Welcome to Little Falls. I'm happy to see you all. We weren't sure we'd find you after our communication got shut off."

We all glare at this man. I go to say something when Chris cuts me off. "There were more of us before they got butchered." His voice is full of venom. Chris hasn't really spoken to me much, and I'm shocked at what he just said. My head snaps over to him. The man's once cheery-looking face changes, his eyes lower, and he looks over at Chris. The hair on the back of my arm stands tall at this, and it puts me on edge. He appears to ignore his comment while shifting his gaze toward me.

"Most of the time, they associate themselves with each other, making a type of family, if you will. Now every house handles maintaining themselves and everyone is expected to contribute. But if the female wishes to take on more of a homestead role, that is always accepted. "

My mouth falls open. "So you mean Harlem?" I speak before thinking and everyone looks at me.

The man nods and continues. "Yes, that sums it up quickly. Since you arrived with these three men, they will be placed with you, and the younger ones will be taken to the community housing with the other children." He walks over to me and cuts my wrists free. He does the same to the others and explains to the men who walked us here where to take us. The meeting is cut short with no room for questions or ridicule and I'm stunned.

The guy from before comes over to pick me up, but is stopped by Markus as Owen retrieves me. I wrap my arms around his neck as he does, and we follow along quietly. We part ways with Rose after we make Tommy and Chris swear to take care of her, and we're quickly ushered away, being told to head toward what I can only guess is the housing district of this place.

We're shown to an apartment building. After entering, we are placed on the 5th floor. The apartment is three bedrooms, two baths, with a large kitchen and living space. It's nicely furnished from before, I guess, with lots of windows. After we walk inside, the man closes the door and we just look at each other, not really talking. Owen sets me down on the couch before sitting as well. We all take a place around the coffee table. Markus stands against the wall, breaking the silence.

"What the hell?!"

We all let out the breath we didn't know we were holding before a random clattering breaks loose, trying to make sense of it all.

We run over everything.

How do they expect us to just be okay after they killed everyone?

Are we just supposed to join their little society like nothing happened?

We go on about how secure this place seems and how we don't have any weapons. Owen finally brings up the big thing to my mind.

"So, I guess we're in Harlem now?" They all turn toward me with questions in their eyes and my face turns bright red.

I stutter, trying to get something out, when they all burst out laughing.

"Firefly, baby, your face is priceless," Owen says.

I become even more flustered. "Oh, you guys are asshats!" I say loudly before crossing my arms.

"On a more serious note, this place only has three rooms. Who's going to be butt buddies?"

They look at each other before shrugging.

"You know, we all shared a bed multiple times with you. Why don't you just choose?" At this, I go quiet.

"Well, see..." is all I can muster. We look around the apartment and discover what's there. Seeing the bathroom has a tub, I slowly walk over to it and turn on the water, expecting it to be freezing, but I'm met with hot water. I call out in happiness and strip down, not giving it a chance to fill halfway before jumping in. My body dips into the water and I feel myself relax. Looking around, I take in the room. I look over at the door and see Jack. I feel myself blush and I lower my body into the water.

"The hot water works."

He closes the door behind him and strips off his shirt. "Does it?"

I nod my head as I go deeper into the water, leaving my nose and eyes out. I watch as he strips while continuing walking over to me.

He leans over the tub and dips his hand under the water to my chin. "That feels nice, doesn't it?" he says, my eyes staring at his lips. I squawk out a yes.

"But I can think of something that would feel even better," he says. His eyes look down to my lips and he slowly leans forward.

My mouth parts slightly as I go to meet his, teasing, not even an inch apart. "And what would that be?" I say, my tone hushed, wanting him to close the gap.

He holds it there for a second or so more before meeting my lips. I wrap my arms around his neck, diving deeper into the kiss. He explores my mouth as I do, his kiss going from soft to hard and passionate, all the built-up suspense flooding out in this moment. He climbs into the tub, no longer wearing his boxers, and I feel the water rise. My hands travel over his shoulders to his chest. My nails dig softly into him, earning a soft moan. Moving my hands from his chest to his back, I test the water gelding down his back. I leave sight scratches down his back. He takes in a breath and I stop. He pulls away and presses his forehead to mine.

"Please, Firefly, let me show you what I've been wanting to do since that morning all that time ago." I nod my head before grabbing his hair and pulling him back into me, hungry for more.

His hands travel my body under the water. I feel him go from my stomach down to my butt, feeling every single inch he can, before moving back to my breasts, cupping them lightly and breaking our kiss. Leaning down, he takes one into his mouth, swirling his tongue. I feel my hips buck up and his large member lays flat against my stomach. Rocking my hips back and forth in the water, I feel it slightly graze his member as he moves to the next, giving that one the same intoxicating treatment. He brings his attention back up to my neck and starts suckling there. My head falls back with a large moan echoing around the bathroom. His hands move lower to my ass before scooping me up, lifting us both out of the water. I cling to him as he does. The cold air hits me and goosebumps jump up on my skin. Stepping out of the tub, he goes directly across the hall to what I assume is his room. He walks me over to a bed, not caring about the water that must be soaking it. As he lays me down, my legs sit bent, closed to his view. He opens them and climbs on top of me, kissing down my neck. Yet again he moves down my body, showing every detail attention. Skipping the carving in my skin, he moves toward my center, picking up my left leg. He starts at my knee and slowly makes his way back, nipping and kissing. He watches my reaction as he gets closer; I become more sensitive, squirming with every kiss.

As he reaches my center, he hovers before moving to my right leg. The anticipation is making me wet with need. He goes painfully slow doing the same. He once again reaches right before my center; this time he licks a trail up at my bend where my thigh meets just before I shudder at the unknown feeling. He hovers so slightly that I can feel his breath on my skin before he lightly licks me. I watch as he looks into my eyes, and I squeeze at the intensity that is coming off him. He dives into me, sucking and licking, twirling in all the perfectly tortuous places. My back arches with every movement, wanting more. He slowly adds one finger, and my back raises more; two fingers, and I'm gripping the sheets, my breathing speeding up; he adds one more, and a small pain enters but quickly turns to pleasure. I wiggle at his touch, wanting more. He speeds up his movements and I slowly grab my breast, playing with it. I earn a "good girl" from him and my stomach soars. I feel myself rounding the corner as my breathing increases, I'm right on the edge. He stops.

I look at him, wondering what happened. He roughly flips me over and pulls my ass toward him. I arch my back as I predict what is about to happen. He traces a line from my center to my ass, taking away his hand. He quickly brings me to sit down on my butt. I yelp in surprise and my toes curl. He grabs my hair and wraps it around his hand not once, but twice. Lining himself up with me, opening, he pulls me back. I feel him right at my entrance, teasing me, making me want more. I try to ease back onto him, but I feel a pain explode as I do, causing me to move forward quickly. He leans forward and whispers into my ear, "I don't think I told you to do that, Scarlet." My name is laced with so much lust. I hear his breath as he teases me more. I sit there in anticipation.

He slowly enters me, and I feel the sweet feeling of the stretch as he glides in and out of my soaked core and the moan that comes out of me is long and breathy. He rubs my ass as he goes in and out, slowly building speed. His full size hits every spot, making me want more, but I'm not sure I can take it. As his pace increases, there is a click behind me, but I pay it no mind. He pulls out and flips me over again. Crawling onto the bed, he lays down and pulls me on top, facing the door. I see Owen 'eyes take all of me in, and I lock eyes with him as I ride Jack. I slowly move my hands around my body as I do, making more of a show for him. I see his hand twitch as he goes to his pants. He unzips himself and starts stroking inside; the outline shows me he's into this, and the way he stares at me makes me go even harder. I feel myself getting closer, and Jack's member swells inside of me. His hands go to my waist and bring me down harder on top of him. I arch my back more, my hands travel my body, the heat rises in my cheeks, and I feel myself climb even higher. My toes curl and all at once everything tightens. With one final slam into Jack, everything unravels. I let out a scream as everything explodes into bliss. Jack grips onto my waist, keeping himself planted. As he finishes, I feel him fill me from the inside and Owen steps outside. He pulls me back into him. Pulling out, he lays me on his chest. Our breathing is fast as we both calm down. The excitement makes me tired and exhausted.

"I never even got to clean myself, asshole," I mumble, and I feel him laughing. I smile sweetly, and he kisses my forehead. We chitchat about random things, filling the quiet void around us.

# Chapter 21

## Scarlet

After a couple hours, I get out of bed. Jack dozed off, and I slowly peel myself from him, making sure not to wake him up. Going back to the bathroom, I pick my clothes up and throw them on quickly, running my fingers through my hair. I head out the door and down to the street, making my way to the place where we had entered. I see people, actual real-life people, not baffling or irrationally damaged people! Some people walk around in pairs while some are in groups. I stop one of them by getting their attention.

"Excuse me!"

A girl turns my way and pulls on her walking companion's sleeve.

"I just arrived today, and I don't know how anything works. Can you help me?"

She smiles brightly at me, and her brown eyes slant slightly, seemingly happy to have met me. Weird, that's a reaction I haven't gotten in a while. I feel myself warming up to the stranger already, and a sense of familiarity washes over me. "Yes, of course! All you do is go to a shop and they should have your work hours tallied up and available! You can see the commander of supply about how much you'd like listed in each one, and once you get your items, they will subtract how many hours your haul costs."

My face must show my confusion, so she continues.

"Silly me! So, you gain hours by doing jobs around the settlement. Laundry duty, for instance, for every one hour of work you earn 30 minutes. They have them listed on the job postings. But when you first arrive, your household has 30 hours available in each store to get you started and each item will tell you how much of the time it will take away. It's a little confusing. I think they have it posted somewhere near the shops!"

I take a mental note and thank them, giving back the warm smile I was given. The tightness in my chest is gone, and it almost feels like the old reality, just with more walking infected things than there used to be. Before continuing on with my scavenging, I see the shops come into view and I walk into what seems to be a general goods store. Slowly, trying not to draw too much attention, I go to the first shelf lined with various canned goods salvaged from the outside. On a little wooden sign, it reads *Canned Goods: 5 minutes per can*. Unique items cost higher or lower—pots and pans, dried goods, meats, they have it all. I walk to the counter where a homely lady stands, and she smiles at me.

"Hi, sweetie, what can I help you with?" She says, a Southern accent strong in her voice.

I speak softly, feeling out of my element. "Hi, we just arrived and I'm kind of lost in this whole settlement."

She smiles brightly at me before pulling out a sheet. She asks me where I live and I tell her the apartment number. With an "ah-ha," she points to my number, and it reads "Apt. 502 – 30 hours."

She explains to me I should have this credit in all the stores separately and to get what I need to set up our home. I thank her and let her know I'll be back once I get my group with me.

Looking to my left, there's an enormous billboard beside the entrance, and it shows different jobs you can sign up for.

Jobs coming up, please see commander of supply for more info.

Laundry - 30 m per hr.

Water supply - 2 h per hr.

Kitchen team - 1 hr. per hr.

Inventory - 30m per hr.

Field team - 2 hr. per hr.

Search and retrieve - 3hr per hr.

Scavenge team - 5hr per hr. (shift and finds depending).

And the list goes on. It seems like you have to be productive to the settlement to earn and buy items. I walk around for a while, looking at everything, taking in how they have items you wouldn't think of needing. Towels and such are something else you must earn. So they give you the house, but nothing else. Good to know.

I go to return to my new home and share what I've learned, but as I enter the building, I notice a shadow following me, looking over my shoulder as I walk toward the stairwell. I can't help my heart as its pace speeds up. I stop right at the door. The footsteps continue at a fast pace and my palms become sweaty. Someone grips my shoulder and I grab their arm, using it to slam them into the wall beside me. My eyes search their face, and everything stops.

My heart beats loudly in my ear as I slowly slacken my grip, and tears spill out.

Ralph stares at me, his eyes wide, his shoulders shuddering as tears well up. He grabs me and we embrace each other for a long while, saying nothing. His age is showing even more. The beard he grew makes him look even rougher than before, and he's lost a lot of weight. We just sit there holding one another.

"Dammit, firecracker, I thought we lost you back there. I almost beat Tony to a pulp for leaving you. I promise we doubled back every day waiting for you."

I stare at him and shake my head, wiping away the tears.

"No, I told him to go. I tried to meet you on the road, but then I ran into this group and so much happened. Ralph, God, I'm so happy you're okay. How did you end up here?"

He explains how they saw some signs up about Little Falls and thought I'd find my way here. The other guys made it, and they picked up some along the way. "God, Thomas and Chris are going to be so excited. We have to go find them." In all the excitement, I agree, and we head back out. We talk about stuff we've learned, he tells me about what they call a brute, the pure size of them, and how they almost lost Chris because he couldn't stop making jokes. We round the corner of the apartment and head toward the street. They got settled in a house because the apartments just recently were recovered when they extended the walls.

As we approach, I slow down. Ralph stops a few steps ahead of me, asking what's wrong. My stomach ties into knots at the thought of how this is going to go. The first person I see as we approach is Tony. He jumps up and, in his own fashion, starts yelling a string of curses at us. Chris comes out the door telling him to shut up, but his face reddens when Tony points at me.

As I stand there strangely, Chris bounds down the stairs and runs right at me. He scoops me up and twirls me around. I laugh loudly, as if he won't drop me. I yell out, "You're crushing me to death!"

My voice is lost in the laughter of seeing my best friend. "We can't lose you again if you can't walk away."

He confirms the death grip, hugging me close. After a few minutes of joy with me and Chris, Ralph taps my shoulder and I look at him. He points to the porch and there, in all his teddy bear glory, is Thomas. He's gotten more muscular, and his hair has been cut. His eyes slowly brighten as I stare at him. This man that, within a few short weeks of the beginning, caused me to trust him and caused my heart to open wide. I push away from Chris, scrambling on the ground from the fast releases, and we run at each other. I jump into his arms. He holds me gentle but firm; he twirls me around and I refuse to unlatch myself from him. My arms still latched around his neck, he pushes me back slightly and looks me over for injuries. "I'm so sorry. If I went with you, we'd never have lost you in all the chaos. It's all my fault. God, it's so amazing to see you. I knew you'd make it back to us."

After a while of reassuring him I'm okay and alive, leaving out the events of the recent past, we just stand there holding each other.


Someone clears their throat, and I turn to see Owen, Markus, and Jack standing with their arms crossed.

Markus looks like he could kill, Owen is staring daggers at Thomas, and Jack's veins look like they are about to explode. I try to introduce everyone, but before I can, Markus is the first to move. He walks toward us, never taking his eyes off Thomas. Grabbing the back of his shirt, he slams him into the dirt and starts hitting him. After two solid hits, Chris slams into his side, his legs curling behind him in the air as he flies. There is a bunch of commotion as everyone yells at one another, but I try to get Markus to stop.

He ignores me. I grab onto his biceps to pull him off. Just as Jack comes into view, he throws me over his shoulder, stopping me from what I'm trying to do. I pound on his back, yelling at him to put me down. He marches away. Owen grabs Markus by his shirt, hauling him after us.

I let out a string of curses, screaming at them to put me down, asking what the hell is wrong with them. They don't say a word until we get to the apartment. As we enter the living area, I pull myself over Jack's shoulder and land right on my back, nearly knocking the air out of my lungs.

"What the actual hell?!" I yell at them, using the counter to rise to my feet. My lack of height, at just 5'2", doesn't stop me from standing my ground.

They all look at me, pissed.

"So, what, you get into society and just leave us behind? Is that it?"

I'm visibly taken aback at this. "Huh?" My face scrunches up and I know they can see my confusion.

"We haven't even been here for a whole day, and you go join another group. So much for loyalty," Owen says, the hurt clear on his face.

I shake my head and press my fingers to my temples.

"So, you all are jealous? That's what I'm reading here."

Their faces go red, and they look at each other for a moment.

"No," Jack answers hesitantly.

"For your information, that was my group I was in before you all. That guy who tackled you is my gay best friend, the older man is like my father, and Thomas is the person who protected me multiple times. Maybe next time ask before you go wailing on people. I can't fucking believe you dipshits! Do you really think that little of me? That as soon as the chance presented itself, I'd just pack up and say, 'See ya'?!" I run out of breath and they stand there shocked, blinking at me stupidly. I throw my arms in the air and stomp off to a random room, slamming the door closed, then throw myself face first into the bed and scream into one of the many fluffy pillows.

After a couple minutes, I gather myself from the mattress and walk out the door. All three of them are sitting there. Markus hits the ground with an *oomph* as I sling it open. Looking down at my feet, he still has his arms crossed and looks up at me. "I'm sorry."

I shake my head and step over him. I feel their stares as I walk to the kitchen and open the cabinets, trying to see what all we need. As I make a mental list of what we need to get, it suddenly dawns on me that we haven't seen Tank. I quickly turn to the door. Ripping it open, I fly down the hallway and down the stairs. The guys chase after me as I bound down and out of the building. The street is much less populated, more of a skeleton crew of sorts. Flying down the road, I come to the street where the town center is. City hall comes into view; I fly up the stairs and open the door with force. I'm going so fast I slide on the smooth floor, my boots leaving black marks. Making my way to the office we were brought into, I bust through the door to see Dean and the man who runs this place having a meeting of sorts. Dean turns to look at me and it almost feels as if he's checking me out. The older gentleman seems to be startled. Keeping my hand on the doorknob, I take a deep breath.

"Where is my dog?"

The older gentleman looks at me and then to Dean. I stare at Dean as well.

"Dustin had him." I stomp over to him and grip his shirt. We are inches apart. The man doesn't seem startled in the slightest; he seems pleased at my reaction. A small smirk grows on his lips.

I speak calmly. "Where does Dustin stay?" I cock my head to the side and offer a closed-eye smile, trying not to look like I'm about to snap.

"He's at the barracks by the gate," he says calmly, almost cautiously. I drop his shirt and run out, following my path from before. I run toward the gate. I see a metal door in front of it and I burst into it. As I do, heads turn to me. About seven athletic men, all average-looking, are huddled around something. I see fluffy ears poke up. These seven grown-ass men all are sitting crisscross-applesauce around my Tank as if he's a puppy, doting on him. One has him on a leash, the one I assume to be Dustin. I march over to him, ignoring Tank's big brown eyes for a moment, and snatch the leash from his hand.

I grit my teeth at him and say, "MY DOG!" I bend down and pick up Tank in a firefighter's carry, turn around, and exit the barracks. As I slam the door, I hear boots behind me, trying to catch up. I turn to who I assume is Dustin. He asks me to stop, and I face him. He has a thick Southern accent, deep brown hair with green eyes, and an army-green shirt with camo cargo pants.

"Listen, I'm sorry. I promised I was going to return the little buster, but he's so darn cute and everyone wanted to love him. Few pets made it this far. I promise I had no ill-intent with him." I look him up and down before putting Tank on the ground. The floof of his tail is beating against the ground, and he looks between me and this guy, and his head turns left and right. I grip my arm, rubbing it up and down for some weird reason. I feel embarrassed.

"I shouldn't have been such a bitch. Me and him have just been through a lot and I was going crazy. But next time, don't kidnap someone's dog." For some weird reason, I feel shy, and I look everywhere but at him.

He scratches the back of his neck before extending his other hand and introducing himself. I return with my name, and he compliments me on Tank. "Did you have him before everything happened? A lot of pets didn't make it because these things don't discriminate against who they attack." I explain how I found him on the highway, and we go on this topic for a minute before Owen and the others finally catch up. They shout and cheer at Tank, wanting him to come over, and I tell him to go ahead. Dustin and I watch Tank go love-crazy.

"Well, little lady, if you ever need a tour sometime, you can find me at the barracks. Just ask for me. I know Dean was bragging about your spirit, and we can always use more scouts. It pays well in our little compound too." I look at his face, trying to see some hidden expression, but find none.

"Thank you. I will take you up on that sometime soon. I appreciate it."

I wave goodbye and walk back toward Tank. The guys all stand as I approach. I point my finger at their faces. "I expect you all to apologize, not just to me, but to Chris and Thomas, for being asshats. After you do that, then we can move on with life." I get fast nods before I walk past the group of idiots. Tank cheerfully follows me as we go back to our apartment for the night.

# Chapter 22

## Starting Anew

The sun peers into our new living room. It shines past the gray curtains and right into my eyes. I stretch awake, my back and legs shake as I do. I rub my eyes as I notice something big and heavy lying on my torso. A giant fluff ball, also known as Tank, is snuggled into my chest. His body is too big for me, but he made himself comfortable on the couch and me. I pet his head and he sleepily looks up at me. His big brown eyes give me a pleading look, not ready to start the day either, but I pat his torso three times. "Come on, lazy fluff, we got to go see about this whole scouting thing." He huffs at me, his head shaking as he does. I laugh at his reaction. He grumbles at me as he turns further into the couch. I wiggle my way out from under him and, like the cheery little soldier he is, he prances behind me. I approach the kitchen to see an apple on top of a note.

"Hey, Firefly, we went out, we'll see you later!"

Biting into the apple, I put on my shoes and call for Tank. We make our way down to the main street, I guess you'd call it. Walking past all the surrounding bustle, I figure now's a good time to take Dustin up on that tour and the job offer.

Making my way to the barracks, the smell of fresh bread hits me and my mouth waters. I follow the smell and walk into the general store I was in yesterday. There stands the same homely woman, just as she did yesterday, only she has a fresh-baked loaf of bread on a wooden cutting board. Me and Tank both stand at the counter. He jumps up, his front paws resting on the smooth surface, and he is visibly drooling. She turns around, leaving the bread where it sits, and lets out a thunderous honeyed laugh at us.

"Darlin', are you okay? You and that pooch there seem like you're about to attack me."

I shake my head, leaving my trance, and look down at Tank, who has drooled a puddle where he stands. I check my mouth to make sure I'm not drooling as well, and with wide eyes I look up to find the woman hunched over, enjoying our reactions too much. "So, you're the lady my boy Dustin was talking about. And this must be the sweet little pup he said you almost bit him over."

"I— I, uh…um."

I don't know what to say because this woman holds the bread in her corner, literally, and I think I'd kill to have some. She pets Tank and baby-talks to him for a moment before walking over to the loaf and cutting a sizable chunk out of it. I watch her every move, wondering what she's about to do. She puts some jam on it, spreading it all around before turning around. She bends down into a bucket and pulls out a bone. She places the bone in front of Tank. His eyes go huge as he takes the end of it and drags it off the encounter. She then holds the bread out to me with an outstretched hand.

"How much?" I ask, not wanting to blow all our money on bread… But it would be so worth it.

She laughs a small laugh and tells me to take it. Anyone who looks that wide-eyed at bread deserves a slice. I thank her and bite down. The jam is sweet, and the bread is fluffy. "Oh Mah God," I audibly moan out, my mouth full of the tiny fluffy heaven. I stand there for a second before someone clears their throat, and I turn to see a woman with a basket full of items. Placing a hand over my mouth, I mumble out a sorry and thank the woman before saying goodbye. She waves at me as we both leave, our prizes in tow.

I'm focusing so much of my attention back, I don't even realize there is a body standing in front of me until I hit it, nearly dropping my valued piece of bread. I let out a shriek as I fumble for it and the stranger catches it in his hands. I look up to see Dustin standing there with my delicious treat literally in hand.

I outstretch both of my hands with a desperate look of pleading in my eyes. He looks between me and the bread before holding it out of reach.

"Hey, that's mine, gimme!" I jump at my treat for dear life, and he finds amusement in my struggle.

I stop jumping and cross my arms, giving him a glare.

"Give it back," I say; my threatening tone is very real.

"Are you coming to take me up on my offer?"

I glare at him harder, my pout on display as I switch between him and my bread.

"I was until you stole my bread."

He looks kind of shocked at my answer before letting my bread down, and I snatch it from his hand, grumbling to myself. He licks his hand where the jelly sat in his palm before sucking on his finger, staring at me way longer than necessary.

"All right, follow me," he says, and I do just that. We enter the barracks and I see about 10 cots in the building. He takes a left and I follow him into a tunnel that I guess is the wall they built. We go down a ways, passing many doors before entering at the end. It's like a warehouse: boxes are piled over the area, shelves are lined with items. There is a desk to the left and we head toward it.

The man I threatened, Dean, is sitting there looking over some papers as we approach.

"Hey, Dean. Ms. Scarlet here would like to sign up for scout duty."

Dean looks up at me and lowers his papers. He checks me out yet again, only this time his eyes linger at my scar under my collarbone. Part of it sticks out and I quickly pull my shirt to cover it.

He opens a drawer and pulls out a clipboard. Sliding it over across the desk, I see shifts and locations in a box form. Dustin looks over at them too.

"There is a trip heading out tomorrow to the mall. How about we go together?"

I see only one other person is going and I shrug my shoulders, sign my name, and then thank them before sliding it back over to Dean. He looks over the paper before grunting out, "Go set her pack up. I think Jason has that old equipment for the dog too. See if you can take it down."

Dustin gives him a slack salute before we head back down the hallway. We stop midway to the barracks at a door. He pulls out a set of keys, unlocks the room, and flings the door open.

"Tah-dah!" he sings, flaring his arms open as if to present the dark room. I cock my eyes at him, then the room, and then back. He looks to the left and notices the lackluster luster of the black void. He steps in and flicks a switch. Lights flicker on to show an armory of sorts.

I step in and look around. There are so many weapons here.

"Choose a major weapon, a melee, and then a vest and uniform."

I nod my head in acknowledgement and step forward. Guns line the walls, but looking into the corner, I see a choice of bows. Bending down on one knee, I look through the pile until I find one that is actually my size. The compound bow has a black base with silver accents. I pull back on it to find it weighted perfectly. There is a sight already attached, and I look over the pile, pulling three more. I ask Dustin for a screwdriver and start disassembling them for the parts I want. By the end, I've added a sheath for arrows, a holder on the end, and a better sight.

I quickly look through their arrows, taking twenty of them, and switch out their tips for hunting ones. In that process, I also find a trigger, and I attach that to the bow so I won't forget it. I pick a simple brass knuckle-style blade that's gold with silver.

Walking over to the clothes rack, Dustin helps me find a vest that fits correctly, and I pick out the correct sizes for me. I take a black long sleeve sweatshirt with the cargo pants they all wear and a belt. After gathering all the items, we walk over to a caged area and there is someone inside who we hand everything over to before signing an inventory sheet. Dustin tells him we are leaving on the trip tomorrow and his response is he'll have everything ready by then. After making his way back through the barracks, Tank is quickly lost in the crowd of "good boys" that erupt as they praise him, loving every minute.

"So, I guess you better say bye to your group, then head back this way."

I look at him with my eyebrows pinched together. "Why?"

"We always stay in the barracks before the next day's trip. That way we can load up right away and be gone. Just makes it more efficient than trying to wait on people."

"Okay, I'll be back later, I guess. Come on, let's go say bye-byes." Tank quickly breaks free of the swarm of fans, and we make our way back to the apartment. The sun is setting as we enter, and we make quick work of getting up there.

I open the door to find everyone crowded in the kitchen whispering about something. They go quiet as I walk in and kick off my shoes.

"Hey, guys, is everything okay?" I ask, caution on my front.

They all look to where I'm standing before giving a glance at each other. "We spoke to your old group."

One of my eyebrows raises in question. "And?"

"We explained the situation. Ralph laid into us, but everything is good now," Owen answers before shooting a look at Markus and Jack.

Jack stands to his full height. "So, I know me and you have done some things, as well as you and Markus. I was curious about where we stand."

My stomach dips down to my feet. This is awkward.

As I open my mouth to say something, anything, Markus saves me by explaining.

"Firefly, I know I have feelings for you, and I am quite protective obviously, but me and Jack discussed it, and we are comfortable with an open relationship of sorts, but only between us. Is that something you'd be open to?"

My palms sweat. Oh my god, they are serious. "I mean, yeah, I would. I just wasn't expecting this tonight, especially not before I leave on a scouting trip."

Their faces all drop at this.

"Wait, I'm sorry, what? When was this decided?" Jack asks in his usual demanding tone.

"This afternoon. It will only be for a day or so, and then we'll be right back. And Tank will be with me," I say, trying to lessen the blow. They look between Tank—who is currently trying to catch his own tail; thanks, dude—and me.

After talking them into letting me go without an issue, we sit and enjoy each other's company for a while before I need to leave. Giving Owen and Markus a hug for good luck, Jack hugs me and kisses me. I tense at this but slowly relax, understanding this is a thing now.

Throwing on my coat, I call out to Tank, who comes bounding around the corner and almost plows into me. We head back to the barracks. The streets are dark except for the lights coming from inside other people's homes. I watch Tank's fluffy form weaving back and forth on the road. Passing city hall, I notice most of the lights are still on, but quickly dismiss it. A crash comes from beside the building in an old alleyway. I slowly walk over to it.

I shake my head. It's not worth it. Not everyone's problems are my own.

We finally make it to the barracks. I knock on the door and it thunders when I make contact. I pull back, grinning at how loud that actually was. Some stranger rips open the door; he stands shirtless with some Po pants on. My face turns red as I struggle to maintain eye contact. Putting my hands behind my back, I fiddle with them. Tank trots right by the man like he owns the place, and I force myself between the stranger and the doorway. The man doesn't move as I do this, and I brush up against him. Embarrassment flares even more and I squeak slightly. He tenses his arm at that, and I make quick work of getting away from him. I see Dustin lying on top of a cot, a book laying open on his face as he snores away.

I whistle at Tank and nudge my head toward Dustin. He takes my command and runs.

Jumping onto the cot, he lays his weight paws-first onto Dustin's chest and takes his book into his mouth.

"Guys, I said to f— Oh my GOD."

He rolls off the cot in a panic and the room erupts in laughter. Tank bounds back onto him and starts licking all over his face. I hear sputtering and see legs kicking in the air. I whistle once more to Tank and his cute fluffy head pops out from where it was and turns. Whistling again to signal his return, he jumps on the cot and uses it to fly a short distance before prancing over to me, proud of his deed. I get down on one knee and praise the good boy. Dustin appears from the floor, his hair covered in slobber. I smile brightly at him, giggling at his new hairdo. His eyebrows scrunch together as he tries to restyle his hair, but he lets out a gag when he contacts the new hair gel.

"Seriously, man, I didn't know we were that close."

Small comments break out in the barracks, and I walk to Dustin with my fur missile on my heels. Offering a hand, he takes it and I get the slobber on me, wiping it down my pants. I grin at him.

"Sorry about him, he was just so excited to see his dog-napper."

He laughs at my comment, and we catch up on the plan for tomorrow.

He tells me where my cot is, and I walk over. There's a bag at the foot of the bed. There is a patch across it that reads *Scar*. My hands touch the patch lightly and I smile at it. Such a small thing, strangely, means a lot to me. It's a stark contrast to the project number I was assigned all those years ago.

"The guys worked on that for you. Hope you like it."

I look behind me while still clutching the pack. "I love it, thank you. Do I need to change now or later?"

He points me to a room where I change into their "uniform," I guess you would call it. Walking out, I'm adjusting my belt when I see someone bending down whispering to Tank.

"He's a really great pup," I say. The man looks up at me for a second, never stopping the ear scratching he's giving my fluffy companion.

"He reminds me of my Donald. He passed shortly before all this happened. And I'm honestly kind of glad. No animal deserves to live through a war, especially not one we can't escape."

I feel sadness in his voice. He takes a bag that lies beside him and hands it to me. I take it with a thank you and open it. I pull out a harness, collar, and leash. They are gray, which is a contrast to Tank's black and brown fur. I look at the man, asking a question with my eyes.

"They belonged to Donald. Couldn't bring myself to leave them when I ran. Felt stupid on the run, but now I know he was looking out for your pooch here."

Pulling the harness out, its four points with metal clips reminds me of Kevlar. There are little bags on the sides, and they have some treats on one side. I put the harness and collar on Tank, adjusting it to his body before stepping back with the stranger.

"Justin." He extends his hand in introduction to me. His name brings a slight sadness to me, but I smile and thank him for the amazing gift, informing him we will use it well.

The morning comes too fast, and before I know it, we're loading up to head out. Dustin, Tank, and I all sit in the truck waiting to roll on, going over the plan once more.

We'll follow the lead vehicle to the mall. Once we arrive, we have to break open the doors and create a tunnel using the cars. Then we will wait on top of the roofs and slowly thin out the numbers; when there are just a few left, we'll go on foot, sectioning off the current area and going one by one through each store, documenting what is where. Then we return home.

Seems simple enough in theory. We hear a honk ahead of us, and we move through the gate, heading out onto the highway.

The trip itself takes about two hours total, and when we finally arrive, the parking lot is scarce with vehicles, which is a good sign, I hope. We park on the sidewalk facing the building. Justin and Dean go over and cut the lock that holds the door shut. They open it just enough for the smell to hit us. Rotting flesh. I want to gag as we take positions. Leaving Tank in the truck is the safest thing for him. I stand there waiting for the signal when a small noise draws my attention. Dustin has a Bluetooth speaker in his hand and is scrolling through something in his hand. He turns the volume up to max and a loud rock song blares out. He throws the device on the ground in front of us and we wait for a minute. I hear loud pounding from inside as I ready an arrow.

"Help me, please, they are killing me!" I lower my weapon and go to jump off my station when Dustin grabs my arm and shakes his head at me. I give him a pleading look.

"Someone is in trouble!"

He presses a finger to his lips and leans close. "It's a banshee, they just repeat what they hear. Whoever said that is long dead." I look at the door and watch as an infected pushes its way through its own skin, ripping it at contact with the metal door. It repeats itself in every excruciating syllable.

What the hell is this? Why can it do that? I shiver as I try to steady myself, pushing a breath of air past my lips as I watch it struggle to get free. It breaks through the door and runs right at the speaker, at which point someone takes their shot and the body hits the ground. Blood pools around it and I hear screaming and loud thunderous footsteps coming toward us.

Taking up my weapon, I pull back and am ready for a shot.

The amount of force from the horde sends the doors flying into our trucks, and we have to be fast at cutting them all down. It only takes a couple minutes as they run into the slaughter, but it feels so much longer. The stench that goes with them is making my stomach twist in disgust.

We jump down from our spots, and Justin grabs the speaker and turns it off. I pull Tank out of the truck and walk over to what they called a banshee. I see where she was a bit on her forearm and the skin is peeling away and her hair is almost completely gone. Her once-pink shirt has turned into a mute color, and she seems to be in her teens. I inspected her mouth and eyes, and she seems like your average infected. I place a finger on her neck to turn her head and I feel something hard. As I look at it more closely. I see a shell encasing her throat. It resembles a mass of thickened skin. Callous almost, but red. Using my knife, I chip away part and pull it back. It releases pink flesh, not the normal state of decay; this seems healthy almost. I stand back up and wipe my blade, placing it back in its holster. I let the guys walk ahead of me and we accept the rear. Dustin walks beside me, gun in a relaxed position.

"Creepy, huh? When I first saw one, I had the same reaction. My group ran to help, but they were ripped to shreds by a teenage girl. The way it repeated their cries for help, it felt like nature was mocking their suffering." I place a hand on his shoulder and squeeze lightly. I can't imagine seeing that.

We do the routine rounds, going through the stores and labeling what's left inside. They seem to be mostly untouched, which is great. As we finish up on the first floor, we meet at the stairs and head up together. Paper and trash litter the area. We head to one of the far stores. One guy cuts the lock and starts lifting it, only to be interrupted by Tank. His haunches have grown around his collar, and he growls a fierce sound. His lips curl as he lowers to the ground into an attack stance. I look down at him and squat. I pet his head and look to where he has directed his full attention.

"What is it, boy?"

He growls louder at the gate. The guys look at me, wondering what's going on. "He whimpers at normal infection. I don't know what this means," I answer a guy named Calvin, I gathered from the conversations before. Walking over to the metal sheet, he has an attitude about him.

"Is the little mutt scared?" At this my blood boils. I stand up with my fist clenched by my side. I make my way over to him. Closing the small space, he slams his fist against the metal sheet. *Bang*. I stop in my tracks. "Little puppy's afraid of being a little infected." My gaze falls dark, and I feel my temperature rise. Everyone tells him to stop, but he doesn't; he actually gets louder. *Bang!* "Come on, scary infected people, don't want the baby peeing inside." *Bang!*

Dean grabs him and slams him against the railing, telling him to knock it off. Just as he does, a loud, airy roar breaks behind the gate. Something hits it from the inside and Tank takes a step back, as do we all. The gate shifts up to show a pair of tennis shoes covered in old blood. I feel frozen in place as another roar breaks out. The infected pushes its torso under the gap and charges out of the store. It's running straight for me, but it doesn't seem like it has a target in mind. Its torso slams into me, sending us both flying over the rail. I scream as I feel the small burst of air going on my back. I hit the ground hard, and my head bounces off the tile flooring. My pack has my back in a weird position, and my bow is gone, out of sight. I roll off the lump of supplies to my hands and knees. Pulling itself off the ground, with blood oozing out of its skull, a man who was once six feet. Its arms pulse with muscle. There is the same coating along its arms and chest. It seems to have combined with its shirt, becoming a part of it.

The thing lets out another roar and I feel like it shook the ground. I look around for some kind of cover but find none. I reach back to my belt and grab my knife. The beast charges at me, its arms pumping forward. I meet it halfway and we slam into each other. The hit sends the air out of my lungs and my knife clatters away from me. I crawl across the floor to it and grip it. Flipping over, I see the brute has turned its back on me, and I take the opportunity. I jump onto its back and stab my knife into its shoulder, trying to sever the socket. It roars out in pain as I twist and dig deeper into it. It runs into walls, trying to get me off its back. It hits one of the circular pillars and I'm knocked from my hold. I push up to stand against it before taking a deep breath. I hear Tank barking upstairs and my eyes snap to see these assholes watching me; Calvin is smiling slightly. That motherfucker.

I don't notice the infected run at me, but I feel it as its hands clamp around my biceps, its nails pierce my skin, and I feel the sharp pain as it digs deeper. It pushes us until I contact a wall. My head bounces from the force and pain breaks out on the back of my head. It roars in my face and I can feel its spit. The smell that fills my nose is disgusting and I fight back the urge to puke. It sniffs around my face as it holds me still. It seems to no longer view me as a threat for the moment, and its grip weakens, its face relaxes. I grip the handle of my knife and plunge it deep into its neck, pulling the blade back out as I go to hold my wound. Weird. I use all the strength I can and kick it, causing it to stumble back. I launch at the beast, and we fall together. I plunge my blade right between its eyes, pull it out, then plunge again. After I'm satisfied it's dead. I push off its chest and notice I'm covered in blood. I open my arms and let out a loud scream, "Fuck you, Calvin!" I lower my gaze and settle on the group. Dustin releases Tank and he comes to me, running over the loft and down the stairs. Everyone looks like they are about to pee themselves, and Calvin doesn't know it, but he's next.

I drop my knife and stomp up the stairs. Everyone parts the waters as I make my way past them, straight to the asshole who caused this. I raise my hand and backhand him. The noise echoes through the loud building, and he does nothing. I walk back the way I came and down the steps, grabbing my pack and weapons off the floor. I step over the body of the mutated brute and walk to the trucks, muttering under my breath.

After a while, they finish up. Dustin jumps into the driver's seat and turns the truck on. He turns to look at me and places his hands in a prayer form. "What the fuck?"

I look at him with a twisted face. "Excuse—"

He lets go of everything he wants to say. "First off, that was bad-ass as hell. Who the fuck would have thought you could do that? Like, jumping on its back was insane. I couldn't believe it, and that kick action was incredible. How much force you got in those things? Calvin's a dick, but even Dean looked at him and told him he deserved worse. Where did you learn that?" The amount of word vomit that comes out of this man's mouth is hilarious.

I laugh and tell him to drive. We do and the silence that fills the air is welcome.

# Chapter 23

## Scarlet

As we ride past the gate, I feel like a weight had been pulled off my shoulders. We jump out of the truck with it still running, grabbing our bags. I wave goodbye to Dustin and walk toward the barracks. As I approach the armory with my bag in hand and weapon slung over my shoulder, Dean runs up beside me.

"Hey, do you want to come out on the next trip to the mall?" He seems to be more friendly with me.

"Yeah, when is it? I still need to get all bandaged up." He tells me about a week from today, so the scavengers can get everything out and we can block that one off.

I walk up to the counter that's been cut into the wall with a metal chain-link fence. I place my items and I bend down to pull off Tank's. I leave the collar though, and I place all of it together. A guy who looks to be in his early 20s turns around; scrawny build, glasses that have been taped together from a previous break. He pulls out a clipboard and asks for my name and a full inventory of what I have selected.

After going through the list with Tank's inventory as well, he tells me next time to grab my bag directly from here instead of the barracks. I thank him and head back to the apartment. Tank trots in front of me and we climb the stairs. He waits eagerly at the door for me to open it. We walk into my new home. Opening it, the lights are all on and it's cleaner than when I left. I kick off my boots and remove my jacket, placing it on the island, then round the kitchen to find it empty. "Hello?' I call out.

I hear a stampede of feet, and someone slams into a wall, and a string of curse words come out. I walk toward the noise and end up in front of the room that I assume is Jack's. I open the door and my smile falters as I see Jack struggling to get his pants up.

There in his bed is a woman. She has dark black hair with looks that outshine mine. Her figure is slim and boney, almost. Her eyes show surprise, and she jerks the sheets up to cover herself. "Scarlet, I didn't think you'd be back so soon. They said it would be another day. "

Jack steps in front of the woman, his enormous chest blocking my view.

"I didn't know you had company. I'm sorry."

I turn on my heels and I have a pain inside my chest that I can't place. As I turn out the door, Jack grabs my arm to stop me. When his grip closes around the wound that the brute caused that has not yet fully healed, I yell out, and Tank's haunches go up as he lets out a warning growl.

Jack lets go of me and asks what happened. The deep indentations are still an angry red from healing. I glare at him as I throw on my boots and grab my jacket.

Opening the door, Tank goes out first. I turn to see Jack standing in the living room, no shirt, and his eyes show something, but I don't care to see into it any further. I slam the door shut behind me and walk down the hallway.

My eyes sting, wanting to cry, but I breathe deeply. My lips tremble as I do. "Scarlet, you're home!" I look up to see Owen coming toward me. He goes to hug me, but my arms are wrapped around me, and I step back from his affection. He stops, his arms still inviting me in for a hug. "What's wrong with Firefly?"

Shaking my head, I feel the tears threatening to spill over. I look into his eyes and smile softly. "Oh, nothing, Jack just reminded me of my place. I'll see you around."

I move around him and down the steps. I walk calmly out of the building until I turn a corner, no longer being able to hold the hurt together. I bolt across lawns and streets trying to get as far away as possible. I see Ralph's house in the distance and I turn toward it. Thomas and Chris are on the front porch and they stand as I approach. I bound down the walkway and up the stairs. I throwing myself into Thomas's arms, wanting some kind of comfort, any kind. He hugs me tight before slicking down my hair, no doubt covered in sweat from the trip. He holds my face, and concern is written on his.

"What happened?" Chris has his hand on my back, rubbing a soothing circle.

"I came home from a scouting trip to see some girl in bed with Jack. He didn't even try to hide it."

The tears break loose, and Thomas scoops me up in his arms. They take me inside, where I remain on the couch wrapped up in a blanket, my face red and puffy. Chris is snoring with his head on my lap, and the blanket cascades over him as well. I hear Ralph and Thomas in the kitchen, but I can't make out what they are saying.

A couple hours pass, and Chris explains to Ralph what had happened. He tells me to stay here for now until we can figure things out. I feel so stupid to think they'd only want me. When we were out there, it was easy to think it was perfect, but here, the options have opened, and I'm not the choice for him or any of them. The images in my head of them make me feel stupid, and I curse at myself for allowing myself to think like that.

Loud steps bang on the porch outside and the doorknob rattles like someone was about to barge right in. My head snaps to the door and so does Tank's. Thomas pokes his head out and goes to the door. He cracks it open and whispers something harshly at the person as my head cranes in the direction.

"Scarlet!" I hear on the other side. Jack's voice breaks my heart all over again. "Listen, I can explain. Really, just let me."

Chris is still asleep on my lap. I lift it so as not to wake him and I rub my palms on my pants and wipe my face. I straighten my hair and walk toward the door. Thomas lets me open it. He doesn't move from his spot; his tall and muscular frame hides me well, and I plaster all the hurt and hatred into my eyes that I can. Jack's features soften when he sees me, and realization hits even harder as he takes in my face. "And what's that?" I say slowly, holding my chin high. I wait.

"There's no excuse. It was a stupid thing to do." I cock my eyebrow at him and pull on Thomas's shirt lightly. He steps back as I instruct, causing Jack's face to light up, and I slam the door shut.


Thomas hugs me and I try to settle my breathing.

"That chapter is over for me," I say slowly. Thomas squeezes me in acknowledgment and ushers me back to the couch. I feel the pain in my chest grow tighter, and after a long time, my eyes become heavy.

Darkness.

*"SE-493 Step forward."*

*My body trembles as I do. The white room is blinding and the white scrubs they have me wear aren't helping any. My hair sits in a neat ponytail, flinging with my movements.*

*I fidget with my fingers as the glass mirror sits in front of me, showing myself. The collar blinks blue around my neck*

*"We will begin testing. We will start at lower levels and continue. When the desired effect is presented, the test will stop. Start charge 1." My body jerks and tenses as the jolt hits my neck. After a few seconds, it stops. I breathe heavily, waiting.*

*"Charge 2."*

*Everything is tense and I can't make a noise. I fight back begging. My knees give out, and I hit the floor with a solid thud.*

*"Charge 4."*

*"Ahhhhh!" I let out a cry as my body crumbles into itself. Tears threaten to spill, and it feel like I can't breathe. I claw at the collar they have locked around my neck.*

*"Charge 6."*

*My neck burns at the contact points, and I try to pry my fingers into the collar. I squeeze my eyes shut and let out a scream. My chest doesn't burn like it did that day. My whole body shakes from the blast of energy that hits through the small collar.*

*"Charge 8."*

*When the shock rings through me, I feel like my eyes are trying to roll into the back of my head. My teeth grind against each other and I feel drool seeping out of my mouth. When they release the charge, I yell out. "FUCK!!!"*

*I grip the solid concrete floor and my knuckles turn white and my breathing is getting harder.*

*"Charge 10."*

*As it pulses through me again, my body sends itself backward and I shake, my eyes roll back, and everything cuts out.*

*Out–*

*In–*

*"Ms. Edengrove, your father is here to gather your things."*

*I look at my mother's frail features. Her blonde hair has thinned, and her smile is now gone. There is a tube down her throat, and a machine whirls every few seconds. I kiss her cheek and tell her goodbye. As I stand, I straighten out my skirt and shirt before tightening my ponytail. The nurse walks me to the desk, and there stands my father, his suit ironed to perfection. He looks down at me and a soft smile appears on his lips.*

*"Scarlet, darling, let's go home." He bends down to my level and hugs me as I clutch my bag to my chest nervously. He takes my hand and we walk out of the ICU. I look back at my mother's room, knowing this is the last time I'll see her.*

*Out–*

*In–*

*Come on, we got to run. Austin's grip on my hand is tight, almost painful, as we run through the gray and white halls.*

*Sirens wail out and doors are shutting left and right. The light flashes red and white as we book it to the elevator. He pushes me in first and then joins me, pressing in a code. The elevator counts levels as we go up.*

*When the doors open, the lights are still going but the siren has faded. We run down the hall once more. I see sunlight. My heart slams in my chest. He pulls out a set of car keys and looks for the right one. Stumbling a bit, I dance in anticipation. He gets the right one and swings the door open. We both take off.*

*Sprinting out, I hear a loud crack and look back to see a large wound in his head, blood pooling around it. Yelling rings out. I run back to him and grab the keys that landed only inches away. I unlock the vehicle and bee-line for it, throwing the door open. I force the key into the ignition and the vehicle roars to life. I slam on the gas and promise myself I won't stop. The chain-link fence at the guard post stands in my way. Slamming on the gas, I plow through it. The windshield cracks as it makes contact and I drag it along with me. I hear someone yelling in the distance, but I follow the road to my freedom.*

*Out—*

*In—*

*Kicking my boots and throwing my jacket off, I hear shuffling coming from the bedroom. I call out, but nobody answers. I go to the room where the noise is. I open it. Jack's milky eyes turn to me, covered in blood and flesh. I look down to see him ripping into Thomas. His eyes are lifeless. As he stares at the door, Jack turns back around and continues.*

*Out—*

I fall off the couch covered in sweat. My arms burn and so does my throat. The night sky is dark, and it's just me in the living room. I climb up from where I landed and walk to the kitchen. Grabbing a glass, I open the tap and fill it, gulping the water down. I repeat this two more times until I'm satisfied. I stand there after placing my cup in the sink, clutching the rim of the sink. My knuckles turn white, and I fight the intrusive thoughts that plague my mind.

'You should have just stayed with me. Then you wouldn't have been so attached."

"What did you expect, a happy ending?"

"I expect for you to be worth something!"

My father's voice rings inside my head. I clutch at my hair and shake my head. "Get out of my fucking head!" I yell out loud and I fall onto the wooden floor.

I feel around my neck and find the scar from the collar. The raised skin still lives there, reminding me. I touch the two marks and stroke them softly.

"I don't deserve a happy ending. I caused this all."

I pull myself up from the ground and go for the butcher block that sits beside the stove. I grab a knife and hold it in my hand. The moon reflects off the blade as I place it on my wrist and my body shakes. I feel something cold on my leg. I look down to find Tank. His big brown eyes look up at me, saying something I don't understand. I drop the knife and slide back onto my butt as he nuzzles his head into my arms and whimpers at me. I shush him and pet him, telling him everything that's happened to me. Knowing he'll keep my secrets safe.

# Chapter 24

## Something Is Better Alone

"Thanks, Daniel."

I sling my pack over my shoulder with my weapon and head to the truck. I said goodbye to Tank last night. Justin said he'd watch him for me. I jump into the truck with Dustin after throwing my things in the back seat. I put on my seat belt, and we roll out behind the first truck in the convoy.

Silence fills the air.

"So, I noticed you sleeping in the barracks. Something happen at the homestead?"

I look over at him and release a huff. "When we got back, I was reminded that I'm not the only female here. That's all." He glances at me with a cocked eyebrow.

"One of them was fucking a girl as I walked in. Better?"

His eyes widened. "Holy shit, Scar, I'm sorry."

I shrug my shoulders and place my head on my hand. "It was bound to happen eventually."

The ride is deathly silent after that. The leading truck slows down and parks. Me and Dustin exchange glances. I unbuckle and open the door. Leaning over the top of the door, I call out and ask what happened.

I get a call back that the way is blocked, and we'll have to go through town. I get back in and we turn back to the exit we just passed. Down the roads, the only thing in sight is deserted cars and the trash littering the streets. I feel a pang in my stomach that makes me uneasy.

"I don't like this, Dustin," I say as I look out the windshield, leaning forward. We move at a snail's pace. I take in all the surroundings, looking for the infected that should at least be strolling the road. As we pass a four-way intersection, a scream breaks out and the truck ahead of us fully stops. Dustin and I exchange glances and the hair stands up on my neck.

"Fucking go!" Dustin yells, slamming his hands down on the wheel. We watch as the infected runs at the truck and slams its body into it, causing the truck to rock.

The infected hits the ground on its back. It gets right back up and starts trying to claw the door open. The thuds make us jump with every hit. We watch in horror, unable to go past. Finally, I guess the driver snapped back into reality because the truck moves, but instead of slowly he slams the gas, causing his engine to scream to life. They take off, leaving us. Dustin follows suit and tries to catch up.

We pass the intersection, and I see a horde coming our way. "Shit, Dustin! Fucking drive!" We try not to lose the only person who knows where to go exactly. The infected stumble over each other, stampeding. The sounds are horrid, and I stare, unable to look away.

"What the fuck?!"

Finally snapping away from the horde, I watch as the truck ahead of us fishtails back and forth all over the road. It's too heavy, and he's fighting for control. Because of the abandoned cars everywhere, the back-end clips one and he loses all control of the front. It slings to the left, and the high speed sends the vehicle right through a storefront. We fly by them. Dustin looks back and forth, trying to look and not end up the same as them.

"Fuck! Should we go back? What if they're hurt?" I look behind us and see the horde changing course and running to the collision.

Bodies climb over one another to get to the vehicle.

"They're gone, Dustin. Just get us the fuck out here." I turn away and close my eyes tightly.

"Fuck, what about the other truck?" Dustin looks in the rearview mirror and I try to see as far as possible, but there's no sign of it.

"I think they took off instead of following. We can only hope they're okay." Dustin doesn't slow down until we hit a residential area, finally stopping and throwing the vehicle in park. He leans back and lets out a shaky breath.

I look around before undoing my seat belt. I open the lever and go to push the door open, but as I do, Dustin softly grips my arm. "Wait." I turn and look at him, waiting to hear what he has to suggest. "We need to get back to Little Falls and report."

I nod. "And how do we do that?" I ask.

He lets out an aggravated yell and falls back into his seat. "I don't know. This has never happened. If we can find a map or something. The town was historic, so maybe it's there."

I nod and open the glove compartment, pulling out trash and junk, but no map. "Well, we can't go back the way we came. That place is going to be swarming." He closes his eyes and takes a breath. I can see the panic that's raging inside him, and his voice shakes slightly as he speaks.

"Why don't we look around? Maybe one of these houses has one."

I open the door and slide out. It's probably for the best to leave him to himself for now. Grabbing my pack, I walk to the first house. They all look the same, only this one has Halloween decor that's fallen apart in the yard. I cut through the grass and get up to the porch. The wood echoes beneath my feet. Peering into the window, the house looks like it's been torn through, but maybe there's something they overlooked. I pull out my knife and grip it in my hand, taking a deep breath as the door unlatches. I push it open, and it bangs against the wall, colliding with a piece of fallen furniture. I place my hand to steady it and listen. Knocking the handle against the door, I try to rile up anything that may be hiding, but there's no noise.

Taking slow steps, I turn into the living room and give it a quick check. Papers are thrown around the floor; the couch has been toppled over; the glass coffee table that held decorations is shattered. This house was probably looted. They destroyed a lot of stuff in the beginning. I kick over drawers and bend down, shuffling through the paper. Bills and notes are all that's here.

A photo peeks out from the pile. On the back, in neat cursive: *Dante and Mommy's first trip up north, Age 12.*

Turning it over, a woman is almost smothering a 12-year-old boy with affection. His hair is out of order, and he wears a warm smile. She's draped over his shoulder, grinning from ear to ear. My heart breaks looking around, wondering about the memories they might have had.

I place the photo on the desk and walk toward the kitchen, where shattered plates and bowls litter the ground. Even being careful, my boot still crunches glass with every step. I open the drawers one by one, hoping for a junk drawer of some kind. Silverware, utensils, cloth towels; average items are all that I find. I breathe heavily and continue my search. After looking through the office and bathroom, I eye the stairs before taking them one at a time. They creak under my feet and the dust on the handrail is thick. As I reach the landing, it seems cleaner, not as dug through. I swing open the first door to find a neatly decorated room, red and gray. Dust floats in the air. I walk forward, looking over at two doors: one is a bathroom, the second a shallow storage closet. The nightstands are left untouched, and a neatly written note sits there, folded in half.

The front reads:

## To whoever finds us.

Flipping over the note, I find a cute photo of the woman and the child smiling. She's putting bunny ears on her son.

Dante and I will not make it much longer. The power went out, and those things are getting closer. Dante got scratched today, and I don't think he will make it. His fever is climbing, and it won't slow down. All I can do is give him something to help him sleep through the pain. We were outside looking for a car to take to his nana and pops' since mine got stolen and I didn't want him home alone. One of those things jumped out of nowhere and scratched his arm pretty deep. It's angry, and no matter what I do, it just looks worse. Dante won't make it in this world. He's a kind boy who didn't deserve this. I've seen what happens when someone gets bit by those things, and I can't let that happen to my baby. Please forgive me, God, for what I'm about to do... Please let us rest in peace, and just know my baby wouldn't make it and I would die without him.

I'm sorry Nana and Poppa.

Love forever and always,

Diane Jeffery

Holding the note, I slowly turn and walk across the hall. Opening the door, a woman whose cheeks have hollowed, her skin decaying, lays on a football comforter. Flies buzz around the room. There's a gun on the floor and a crater in the side of her head. Stepping forward, I see a lump curled into her side under the covers, his arm around her waist. My chest tightens and I grip the note. I leave the room, locking the door behind me, placing the note at the foot of it. I take a deep breath, bringing the horror and sadness back down to earth and burying it away. This mother did something no one should ever have to do. Instead of letting her son change, she gave him mercy.

I walk outside the house and sit on the steps. The truck has been turned off and Dustin is walking toward me. He sits down beside me, and I lean back on my elbows.

"Any luck?" he asks. I shake my head and take a deep breath.

"Well, did you know they put them in our packs?"

He pulls the map out of his jacket and gives me an apologetic smile. I glare at him, not wanting to say a word.

"We should camp for the night in the vehicle and head out in the morning." We both agree that it's for the best, so that's just what we do.

The hum of the truck makes me tired, and it's hard to focus on the road. Dustin gives me directions as we head back toward the base.

"Turn left here." Slowing down to make my turn, I roll to a stop. The road is blocked by a few trees. I throw the truck into park and we both get out. This drive is taking longer than expected and nothing appears to be right. I frequently question his ability to read a map, but I'm no different, so we can only hope. The trees blocking our way are pretty tall, but not too bad. I take one side and he takes the other. We haul them out of the way, creating space for the truck. Once we're done clearing, we jump back in and get going. The silence is driving me crazy, but I think he's scared and I'm on edge, so we're not the best travel buddies at the moment.

The focus on getting home is urgent, and we can't run out of gas. We come across a tiny town and I slow down, inching forward on the lookout for any debris. I can't help but think about the incident from before. The sight of countless corpses fills my vision, but I remain resolute in my decision to drive over them. I catch his concerned glance, but his quietude suggests he has no objection. I see a brute on the road. Its head has been crushed in and I try to avoid it, but the back tires clip its leg, and I feel the truck shift. After a few more minutes, the tire light goes off and I curse. I try to go as far as possible before the truck slowly becomes shifted. Throwing it into park, I lay my head back and take a deep breath.

"Can anything else go wrong?"

Dustin agrees and we jump out. "There should be a spare under the truck. Give me a couple minutes and we should be good." I nod at him and send a tiny prayer up to the big man. He works on getting the tire down as I walk around, keeping close but still investigating. I walk over to the brute and kick its arm before lowering myself down to a squat. It's been ripped into and its muscles are torn apart. I check it for anything useful before Dustin calls me over to help. I help him get the bolts loose, taking turns struggling against the steel, and I mutter to myself about bullshit.

"You know, I'd say you're pretty good at handling long, hard things," he says with a mischievous grin.

I stop mid-movement and look at him, raising an eyebrow. "What?" I laugh, trying to make sense of his comment.

He chuckles, realizing the implications of his words. "Well, I just made the connection," he says, his cheeks turning red.

I burst into laughter, unable to contain myself. "Oh, you mean like that?" I tease, playfully nudging his arm.

He nods, his smile widening. "Yeah, exactly like that. You caught me."

We both share a lighthearted moment, the playful banter bringing us closer together.

"Well, you know, I could say the same to you."

He punches my shoulder, and we keep to the task at hand.

"So, tell me, Dustin, why the barracks?" I ask, curiosity piqued.

He rubs the back of his neck, his expression slightly sheepish. "Because I didn't have any females with me besides Ma, and no one grabbed my interest," he mutters, frustration evident in his voice.

Handing the tool back to him, I chuckle. "So getting cozy with the men was better?"

He grins, a mischievous glint in his eyes. "Well, at least they don't nag as much."

We both burst into laughter and continue bantering, the sound filling the air around us. Dusting ourselves off, we make our way back toward the doors.

"Hey, you want to scavenge quick? I want to see what's left. They don't look destroyed, so I'm curious," I suggest. Dustin gazes at the sky for a moment before nodding his head in agreement.

He grabs his pack, and I do the same. We walk across the street and see that the items in a clothing store are mostly gone. Going to the next one, a giant white diamond sits on the window. *Misty's Fine Jewelry.* I try to open the door but it's locked. I look to Dustin, who rolls his eyes and moves me aside before launching a foot into the glass, causing it to shatter. He unlocks it from the other side. The door opens and a tiny bell goes off.

This place has really not been touched, which is surprising. We flick on our flashlights and look around. Beautiful rings and necklaces are all on display under the glass. I shine my light at them but stop when I see a beautiful ring. The stone has a purple and green hue to it, and its band of gold with an interesting design gives off a feeling of nature. I peer down at it. I see a matching necklace that has the same style. Gold with the beautiful stone. The label reads *Alexandrite*. The chain is part of the design, and it almost looks like a choker of sorts.

"Help me find the keys." I look at Dustin, who is looking at watches. He strolls over to me and says he already has them, then brings his handle down onto the display, shattering it. I look at him with a stink-eye before turning around and claiming the beautiful piece of artwork. I place the ring on my finger, and it fits like a glove. I stare at it on my right hand before switching it, so I won't damage it if I get into a fight. He picks up the necklace and tells me to turn around. I do as I'm told, which allows him to clip it onto my neck. It fits just like it thought.

As I run my fingers over the cold, metallic surface, I turn to express my gratitude to him. But in that moment, my eyes catch sight of a looming figure standing directly behind him. Instinctively, I push him to the left, narrowly avoiding the creature's lunge. My arms rise in a desperate attempt to shield myself, but a searing pain erupts through my body. The sensation of sharp teeth sinking into my arm sends waves of white-hot agony coursing through me. With a swift swing to its head, I manage to wrench my arm free from the creature's jaws.

Stumbling backward, my vision becomes enveloped in darkness, tears streaming down my face. The taste of fear leaves my mouth dry as I cry uncontrollably, the pain intensifying with every passing moment. Clutching my injured arm tightly against my chest, my breathing becomes erratic. Disorientation takes hold, and everything around me becomes a blur. I strain to hear Dustin's voice, but it's nothing more than a distant murmur. It feels as though he is miles away, and I am paralyzed, unable to move or think. Suddenly, he lifts me up and carries me back to the truck. Gently placing me in the passenger seat, he hastily climbs in on the other side. But even as I sit there, I cannot calm myself. My gaze fixates on the bite mark, and a surge of panic floods my mind. Will I succumb to the infection? What if Dustin decides to tell everyone if I don't? What should I do? A torrent of questions swirls through my thoughts, each one more unsettling than the last. I have only experienced scratches before, but isn't this wound more perilous?

With a trembling voice, I turn to Dustin, my heart heavy with uncertainty. "Dustin, if I don't make it, I want you and Justin to take care of Tank. Don't let those bastards get their hands on him." His eyes meet mine, his knuckles clenched tightly around the steering wheel.

"It's going to be fine. It's going to be just fine." I feel like he's saying that more to himself than me, but I try to convince myself too.

The pain hasn't gone down in the eternity we've been here, and I can't stop crying out. My body feels like it's on fire. Sweat has drenched my clothes, and my mouth is dry. Dustin keeps looking over at me, and worry continues to grow stronger on his face.

"Dustin, can we pull over?" My voice is scratchy, and the words sound weak. Is this my end? After everything I've been through, *this* kills me, the same thing that I spent years hiding from. I feel the truck slow as we approach another neighborhood. He parks in front of a house.

"I'll be right back, don't move." I nod weakly at his words, and I feel my eyes get heavy. I look around for a couple minutes, but that's all I can take as I enter a sleep-like state. Hearing everything but unable to open or move my eyes, my body is heavy, and I don't control it. Is this how Ryan felt as he turned?

The pain continues to climb rapidly, and it takes everything in me not to scream. I feel whimpers climbing my throat and pushing past my tight-lipped mouth.

"Come on, Scar, let's get you inside." I feel his arms hook under my back and knees, and I feel the sway of his body. Everything around me is screeching and I can't cover my ears to stop it. His footsteps sound like a sledgehammer breaking concrete and my head throbs. He opens a door and climbs stairs before laying me on a cool, soft surface. With my last bit of strength, I cuddle into the pillow and let the darkness chase away the pain that now consumes me.

# Chapter 25

## The Betrayal Born Anew

Waking, my head is full of static and I feel like I've eaten a desert. I look around the room I'm in for a moment and take in my surroundings. I notice the soft gauze on my arms and I peel it back, staring at my wound for a moment, taking it in. It's turned to a scar, and the teeth marks have healed, leaving pink skin in its place. Wrapping it back up, I look around the room. A dresser sits in front of me, with jewelry and photos of the family that once lived here. I see my reflection for the first time, and I look awful. My blonde hair is covered in sweat, making it more a dirty blonde, and it sticks to my face. My clothes have wet marks all over them, and my eyes seem to be brighter. Dirt sticks to my face. Pushing my hair back, I smooth my shirt before throwing off the covers. My pants are gone and I'm just in underwear and a shirt. I look around the room but find nothing. Walking along the cold, hardwood floors, I slowly open the door and hear people talking. I pause, trying to listen.

"She didn't turn. I'm telling you, man, she got bit right in front of me and had all the signs, but nothing."

"Cut the shit, Dustin. We all know that once you're infected, you're done."

He argues again. "Fine, come see for yourself."

I jump into action, leaving the door cracked. I throw myself onto the bed and get back to how I woke up, being sure my bandaged arm is up on the pillow as before. Closing my eyes, I force myself to relax. The footsteps get louder, and I hear Dustin shush whoever he's with. Two pairs of boots approach as the door creaks open. I feel gentle fingers pick up my arm and slowly undo the wrap.

"Holy shit."

In his tone, the unknown voice expresses both disbelief and astonishment.

"See, I told you. Any ideas on what we should do?"

My heart picks up, waiting to hear what they are plotting. "We need to tell Rivers. Doesn't he have that contact in New Jersey? This is information they would want to have."

My heart picks up, and I hear the blood in my ears rushing. They walk out, and I scurry quickly, looking for a weapon. Shifting through drawers, I find random junk. Papers and books, hair ties, nothing of significance. Walking over to the door, I crack it open, and I can still hear them talking. Cutting across the hall, I enter the office. I look through every drawer in the desk and all I find is a tiny letter opener that looks like a long sword. "Shit." I know what I have to do, but I can't leave without my pants.

Gripping the item in my hand, I start down the steps, hiding it behind my back as I round the steps to the living room. I see a candle flickering, and there's shadows in the kitchen. I look for my items and see them in the island's corner, just out of view of the cooking space. I use my right hand and lean against it, poking my head out, and Dustin and the unknown man look at me and shut up quickly.

"Scarlet, you should be resting," Dustin says as he steps closer. My mind races with what to do.

"I– I'm really thirsty."

He smiles as he walks over to his pack and brings out his water, handing it to me after opening it. I drink some of it, resisting the urge to gulp it down.

"Thank you." He nods and places the cap back on it. "Dustin, where are my pants?" I ask and he blushes. So, you blush at removing my pants, but have the heart to sell me out? Good to know.

"You were sweating, so I thought you'd be more comfortable without them." I nod, as if I understand, which I don't. He turns away and the stranger stands.

"I'm going for a smoke right quick." He leaves out the back door, closing it behind him.

"What were you guys discussing?"

He stumbles to find words and I pull out the tiny blade, holding it at my side, not showing any sign of anger.

"Were you two just gossiping about selling me off, maybe contacting someone in New Jersey who is researching this thing?" I ask as innocently as I can.

"Scar— You've got to understand, if there's a possibility for a cure, you're as good a chance as any."

I hum in response. "So, you were just going to sell me for the good of humanity?"

"How did you—" He stutters, trying to figure it out.

"People always do the same. Things. Every. Time."

I grip at the tiny sword; it pinches into my palm and my temper flares. I hear the door open, and both our heads snap at it. The stranger takes in the scene. He charges at me, his shoulder into my waist. I pull back my arm and stab the dull blade into his back in and out. I hear him crying out. We hit the wall, and I crumble. The wind knocks right out of me, and my vision blackens. The little letter tool still in my hand, I raise my arm and scream as I bring it down onto his neck. Blood flies out where I made contact and I hear him choke on it. My hair hangs in my face and I snap quickly at Dustin. His face turns into anger as he stalks over to me. Gripping my hair, he drags me to the coffee table, not even a foot away, and slams my face down. I feel blood erupt from my face and I fall to the ground. I shriek as the injury probably has glass glittered in it. I feel the iron-based liquid pour out of my nose and I smile, looking up at the man I once considered a friend. "You make this so easy."

His confidence fades just enough for me to get the upper hand. I shoot straight up from where I'm sitting and shove him back. He loses his balance and topples over the couch behind him. Grabbing one shard from the table my face just broke, I launch over the couch and land on nothing. A force pushes me, and I clatter forward. The makeshift weapon I was holding goes straight into my stomach and I cry out, tears forming. The pain is intense. I lay there and try to lean forward but scream as it moves inside of me. "You, motherfucker!"

The shard cuts into my hand as I grip it and drag it from my body. Blood soaks the transparent item. He stands there watching me. Blood pumps from my wound and I look at him with the shard in my hand. Using the couch I just launched over, I pull myself up. I feel my body shake as if it's fighting everything. Throwing the glass at him, I scream. Anger and pain fuel the noise, but this one scream is different. The pressure in my chest rises and my throat feels like I'm being ripped to shreds. My ears start ringing and I can't stop. Dustin grabs his ears and blood slowly trickles out. I slam my fist into my wound, causing a strangled cry to break the shriek. I quickly make my way over to him and use my foot to shove him from his squat. His eyes are bloodshot as he looks up at me in horror. I release my hold on the couch so I can stand straight over him.

"Loyalty is something I hold highly, Dustin, but it seems it's just not in your cards."

Looking down at him as I hold my wound, my posture slumps, and I realize that I'm covered in blood yet again. I grab a decorative horse from the side table and stumble on top of him. Bringing the heavy horse above my head, I slam it down and it connects with his face. I do this repeatedly. My side screams and I am completely drained.

I feel myself getting weaker with each hit. I climb off him and try to make it to my pack. The wound on my side is taking its toll and I struggle to pull myself up. My legs wobble and I take a step. My vision goes in and out. I lose my footing as I try to take another step. The floor and I meet halfway, and my face slams off the hardwood, reopening my pouring nose. I use my hands to drag my battered body across the threshold, back into the kitchen. Everything spins, and I can't get my eyes to focus. Looking behind me, I see a trail of crimson where I've dragged myself from. My arms finally give out and the few inches I hold my head off the ground get cut in half. My arms are screaming at me to stop, but I grit my teeth. I let out a loud scream as I try to make it a few more feet. I move my body only inches and it's getting to be too much.

"This is a fucking joke." I laugh to myself as I stretch out a little more, reaching for the thick fabric of my backpack.

My eyes hurt as the fatigue hits harder. Everything is blurring and I stare at my pack, my head falling to the side. It's almost like it's taunting me, only a foot away.

# Chapter 26

## The Bitter Truth

Kicking the rock for the hundredth time, my sister Jenny huffs out air. "Will you stop?" Looking up from my feet, I look her dead in her stupid face and kick it once more. She lets out an aggravated noise and launches at me. We tumble around on the gravel, throwing hits at one another.

"You rat look-alike."

"Yeah, well, the dump called. They want their used parts back."

"At least I can get a call back, you one-night hussy."

We go back and forth, and somehow I get a face full of gravel. I spit it out as I shove her face back away from me. We stay an arm's distance away, both trying to scratch at one another. A loud muffled scream breaks out and both our heads snap that way. We look back at each other before fighting to stand and head toward the noise. Our packs sling as we run back and forth. Jenny is behind me as we make our way to a residential area. There is crashing and more screams. We cut through some lawns and made it to the back door. I look back at Jen and make sure she's really ready for this. Giving me a crude nod, I open the door with my gun at the ready. What I see is a horror show.

A woman is on her stomach with a trail of blood behind her. Blood pools the area around her, and there is a man with his skull crushed in. Walking past her, I glimpse into the living room and see a shattered table covered in blood, a shard of glass dripping as well. A man lays against the wall on his side. A silver stick is lodged into the side of his neck. I look back and see Jenny crouching down at the woman, feeling for a pulse. She touches the woman's neck, and a loud gasp fills the air. The unknown pants-less woman shoves off her stomach onto her butt and scurries back. Her face is cut up, and dried blood covers most of her. Her wound glistens and she looks at both of us with a wild gaze. Her chest rises and falls erratically. I place my hands in front of me, showing her to calm down.

"Hey, it's okay. What happened here?"

She takes another deep breath before forcing down a gulp.

"We got ambushed by an entire herd. After my injury, Dustin brought us here to rest before we returned to Little Falls. But when I woke up, they were acting strange, and one thing led to another, and they attacked me."

Jen brings her close and hugs her, and the woman calms down.

"Where are your pants?"

She looks up at me through hooded lashes and my gut flips. She looks down, and then quickly tries to cover herself.

"That's a good question."

I laugh a little, and Jen shouts at me with a disapproving look. She asks for her pack, so I grab it for her. She pulls out a pair and quickly shuffles them on, releasing tiny grunts as she moves because of her injury. I lift her shirt to look over the wound, and it's deep and red. We wrap it quickly before helping her up. "We have a truck, or at least we should. Why don't you guys come back to Little Falls with me?"

Jen and I exchange glances and agree before helping her out to the vehicle, loading up, and following their map to the settlement.

Made in the USA
Columbia, SC
22 May 2024

35607547R00126